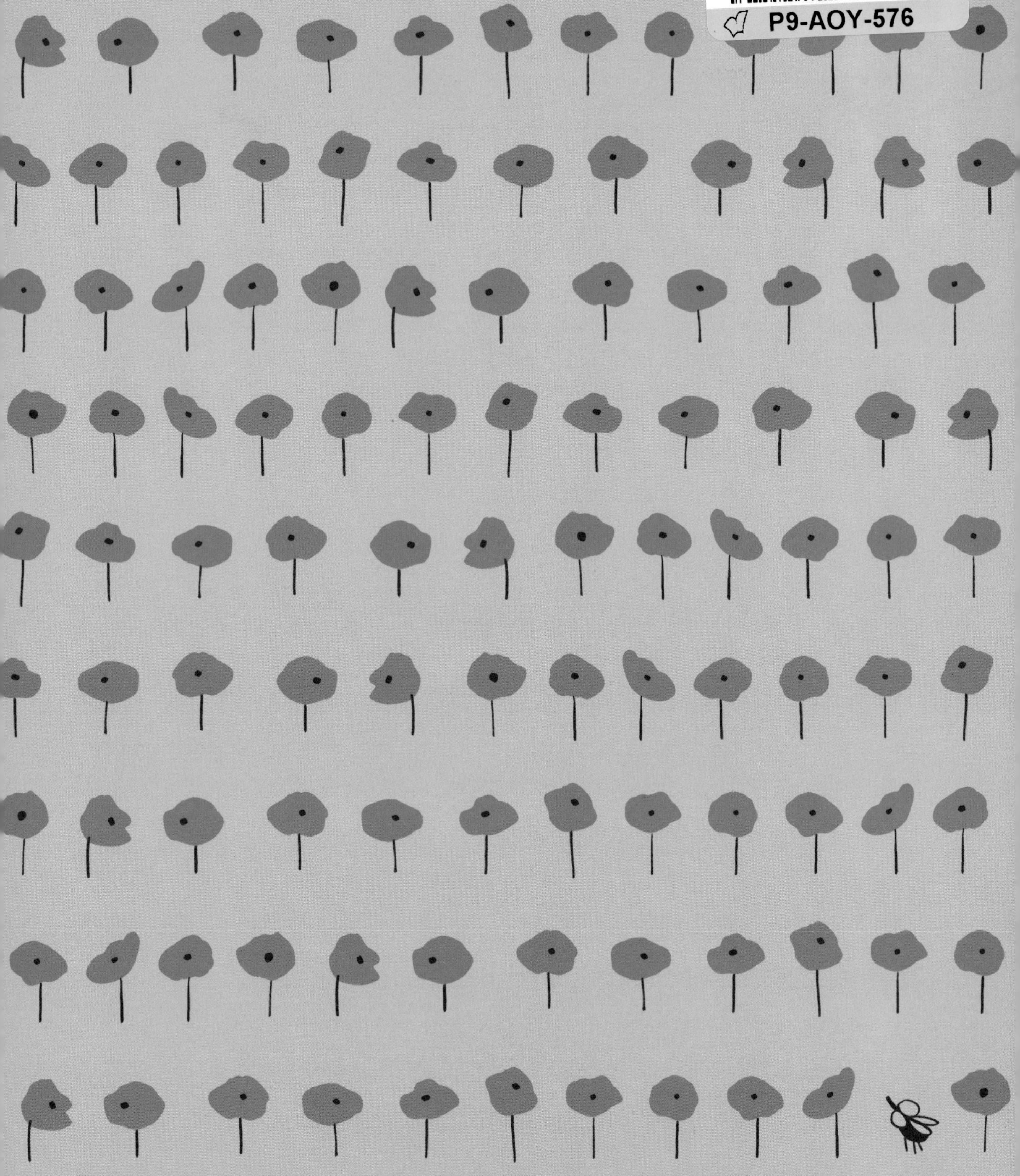

A PLACE FOR

PAULINE

Published in English in Canada and the USA in 2022 by Groundwood Books
Text copyright © 2020 by Anouk Mahiout
Illustrations copyright © 2020 by Marjolaine Perreten
Translation copyright © 2022 by Groundwood Books
First published in French as *Pauline, une petite place pour moi*,
copyright © 2020 by Comme des géants, Varennes, Canada
This edition was published by arrangement with The Picture Book Agency,
France.

Groundwood Books / House of Anansi Press
groundwoodbooks.com

We gratefully acknowledge for their financial support of our publishing
program the Canada Council for the Arts, the Ontario Arts Council and the
Government of Canada.

Canada Council **Conseil des Arts**
for the Arts **du Canada**

ONTARIO ARTS COUNCIL
CONSEIL DES ARTS DE L'ONTARIO
an Ontario government agency
un organisme du gouvernement de l'Ontario

With the participation of the Government of Canada | Canadä
Avec la participation du gouvernement du Canada

Song lyrics: Goldman, Jean-Jacques. "Puisque tu pars." *Entre gris clair et gris
foncé*. Epic, 1987.

Library and Archives Canada Cataloguing in Publication
Title: A place for Pauline / story by Anouk Mahiout ; illustrations by
Marjolaine Perreten.
Other titles: Pauline. English
Names: Mahiout, Anouk, author. | Perreten, Marjolaine, artist.
Description: Translation of: Pauline, une petite place pour moi.
Identifiers: Canadiana (print) 20210369361 | Canadiana (ebook)
20210369442 | ISBN 9781773066097 (hardcover) | ISBN
9781773066103 (EPUB) | ISBN 9781773066110 (Kindle)
Subjects: LCGFT: Comics (Graphic works) | LCGFT: Picture books.
Classification: LCC PN6733.M329 P3813 2022 | DDC j741.5/971—dc23

The illustrations were drawn in ink on paper, scanned,
then colored in Photoshop.
Printed and bound in South Korea

MIX
Paper | Supporting
responsible forestry
FSC® C140526

To my mother, who loved flowers — AM

To Loriane and Carolane, my little
sisters whom I love all the same — MP

A PLACE FOR
PAULINE

Story by

Anouk Mahiout

Illustrations by

Marjolaine Perreten

GROUNDWOOD BOOKS
HOUSE OF ANANSI PRESS
TORONTO / BERKELEY

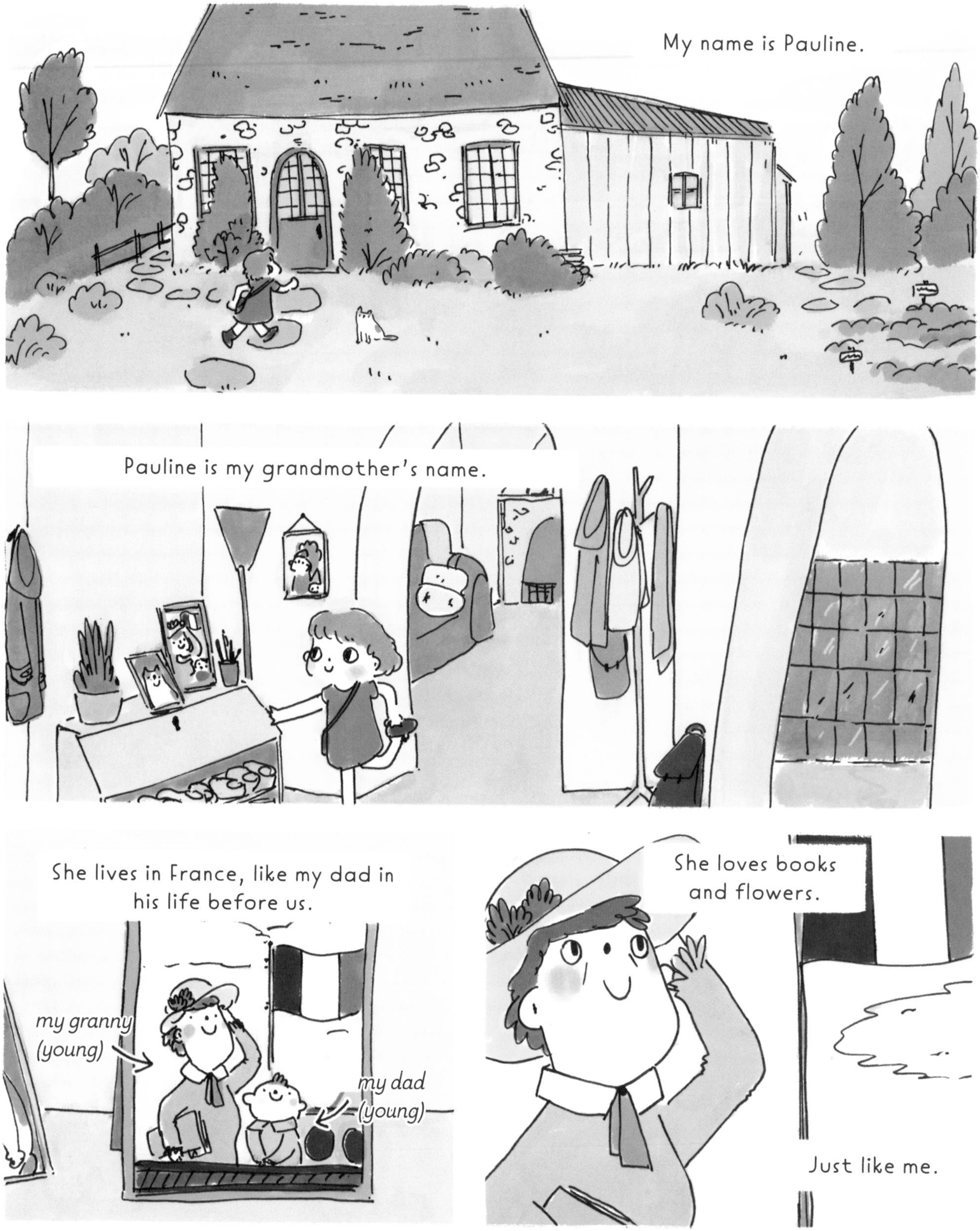

My name is Pauline.
Pauline is my grandmother's name.
She lives in France, like my dad in his life before us.
my granny (young)
my dad (young)
She loves books and flowers.
Just like me.

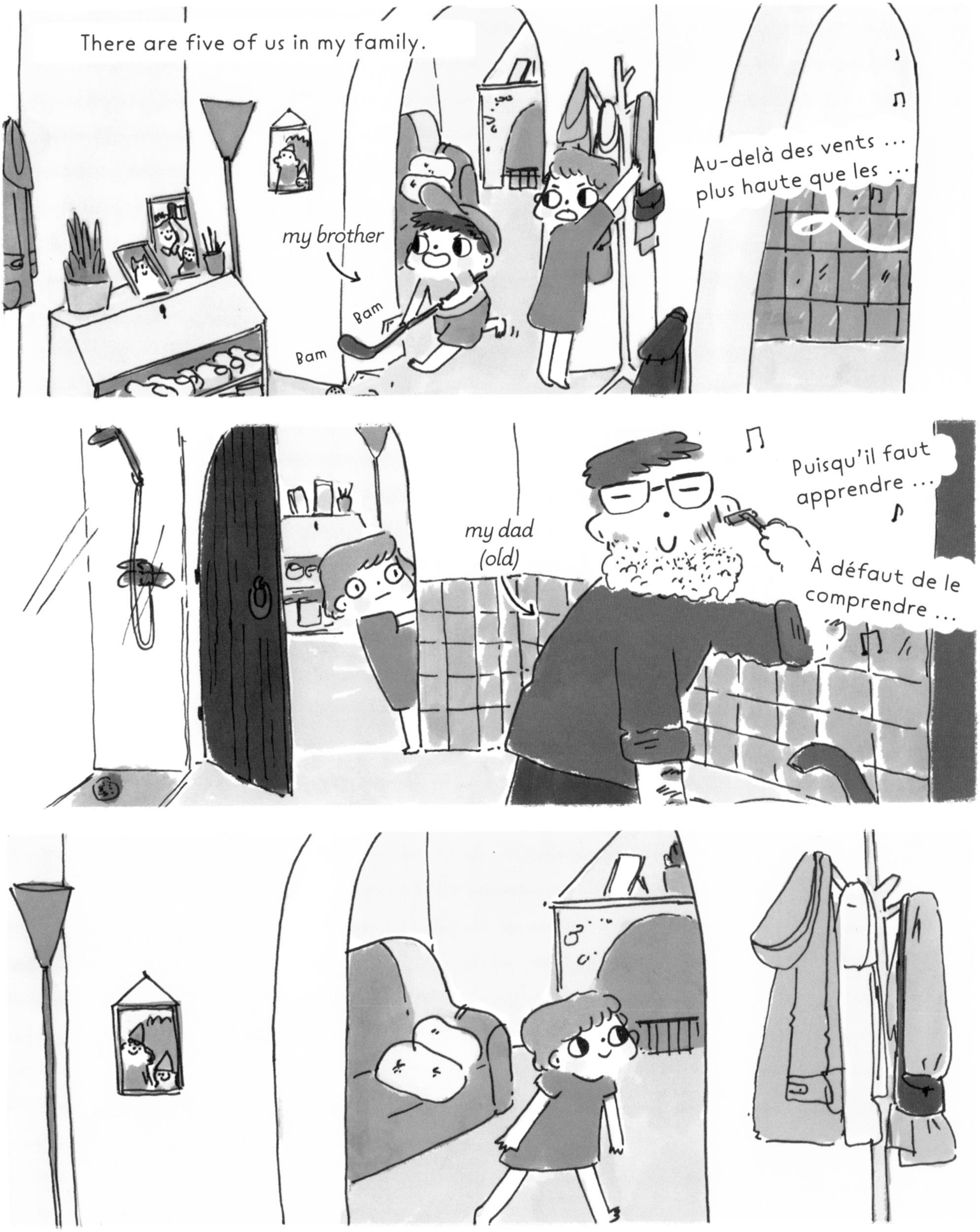
There are five of us in my family.
my brother
Bam
Bam
Au-delà des vents ...
plus haute que les ...
my dad (old)
Puisqu'il faut apprendre ...
À défaut de le comprendre ...

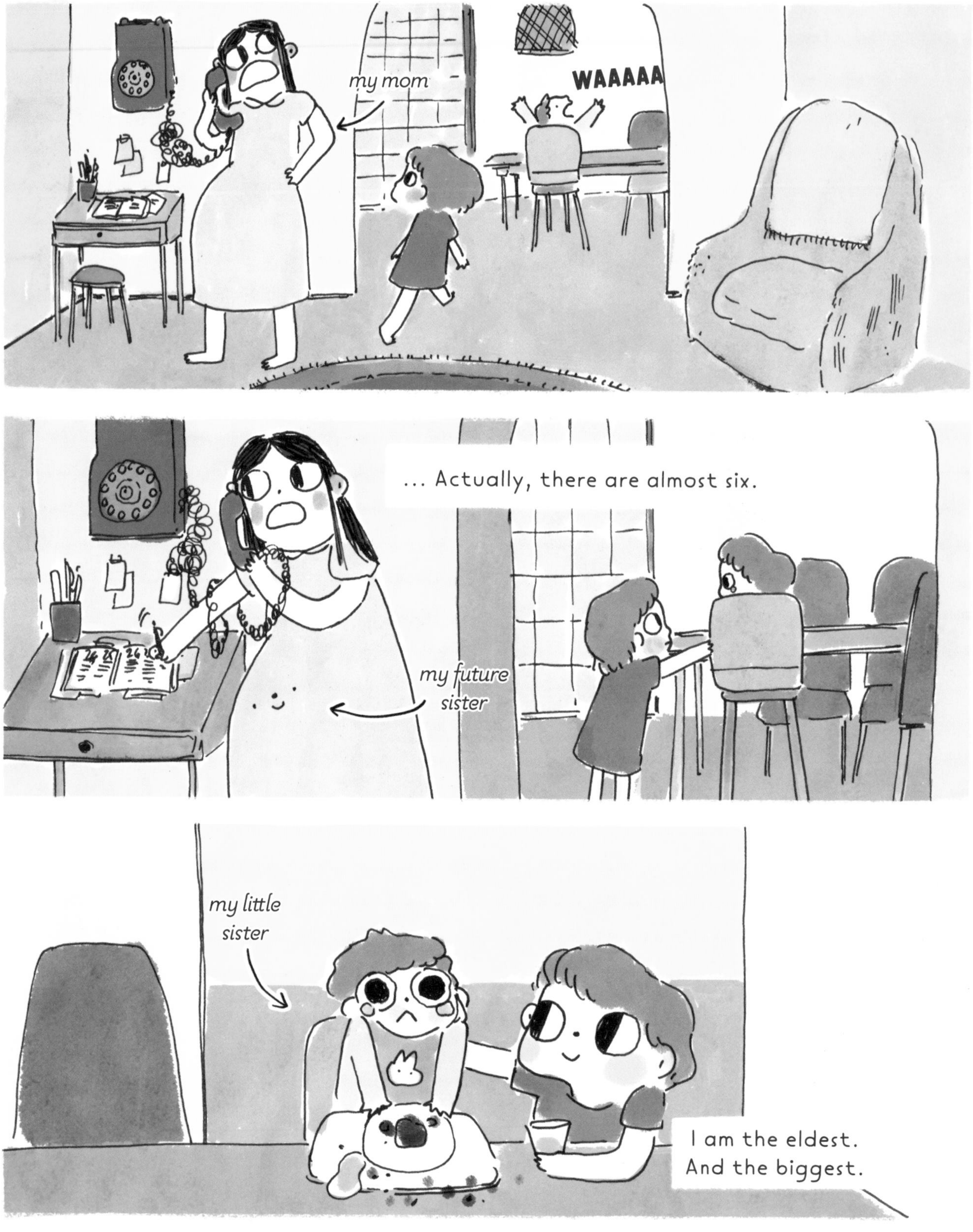
my mom
WAAAAA
... Actually, there are almost six.
my future sister
my little sister
I am the eldest.
And the biggest.

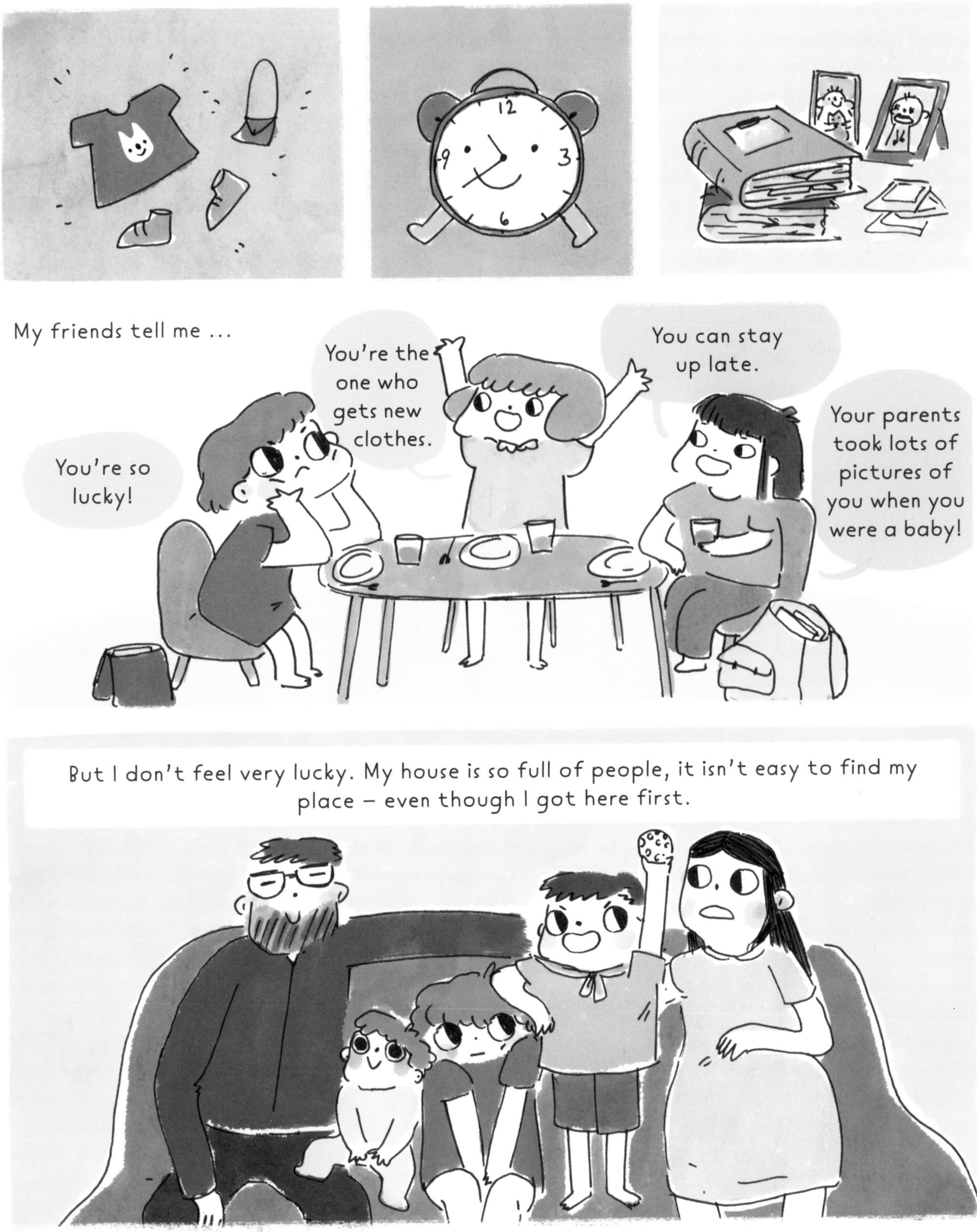

My friends tell me ...
You're so lucky!
You're the one who gets new clothes.
You can stay up late.
Your parents took lots of pictures of you when you were a baby!
But I don't feel very lucky. My house is so full of people, it isn't easy to find my place – even though I got here first.

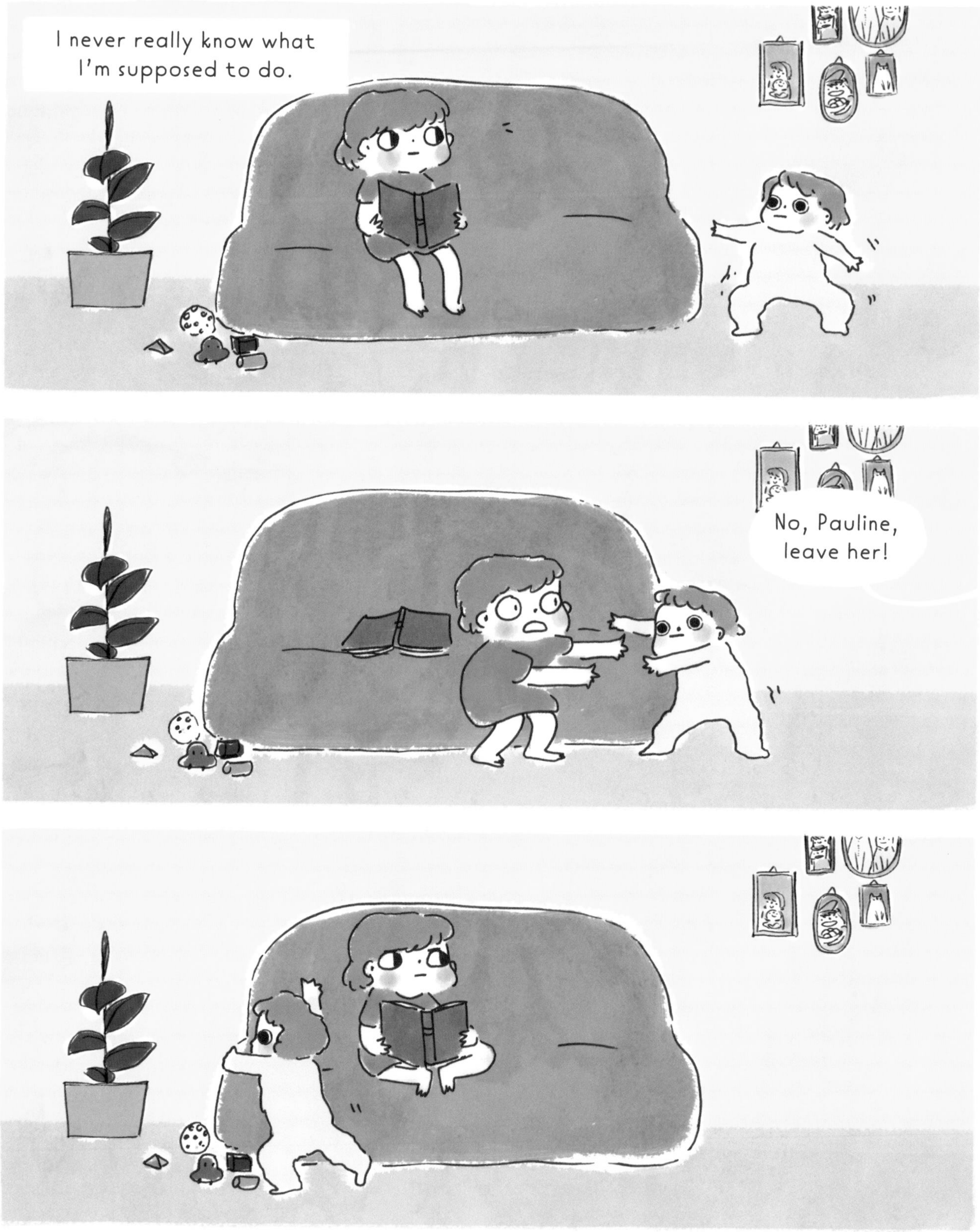
I never really know what I'm supposed to do.
No, Pauline, leave her!

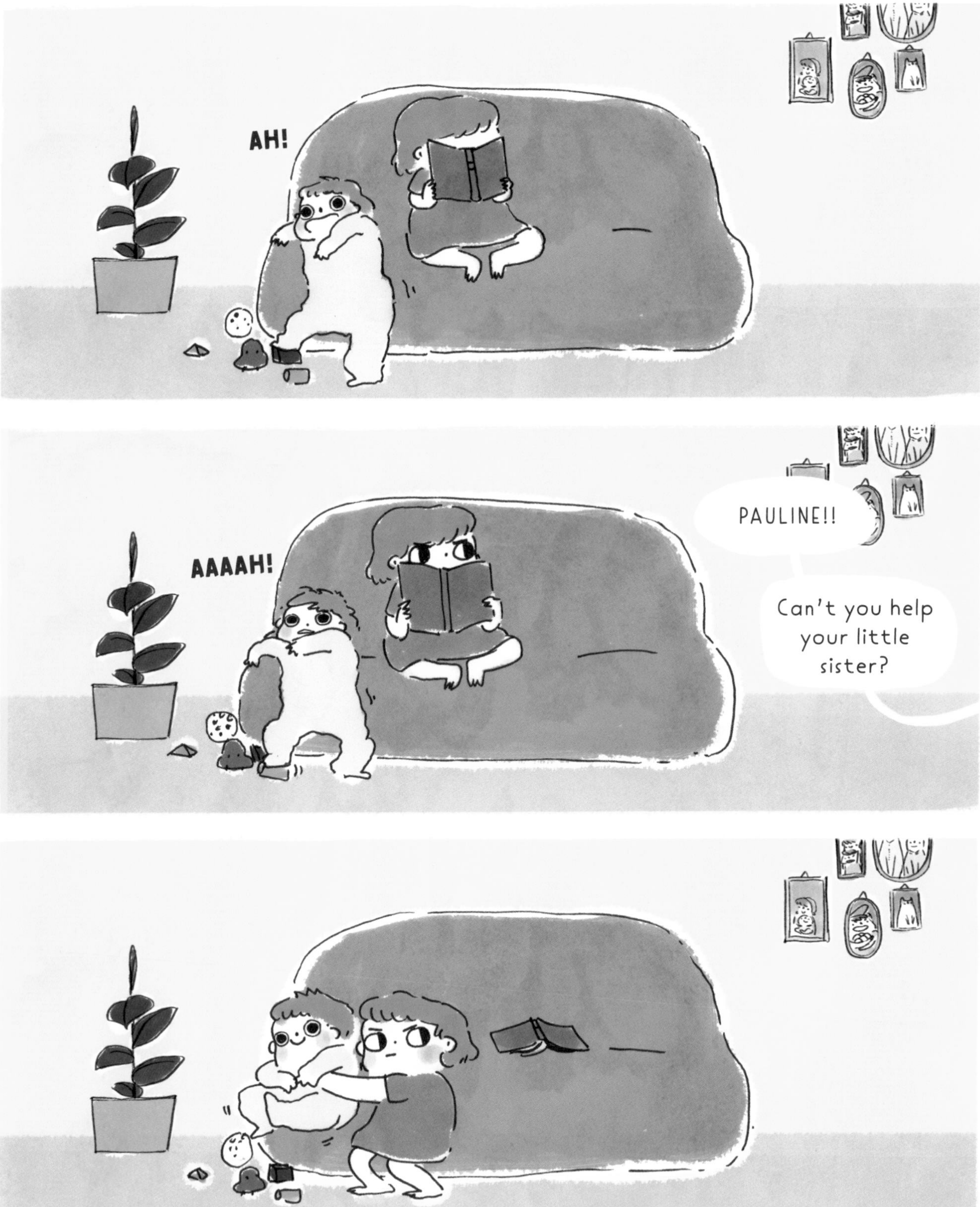
AH!
AAAAH!
PAULINE!!
Can't you help your little sister?

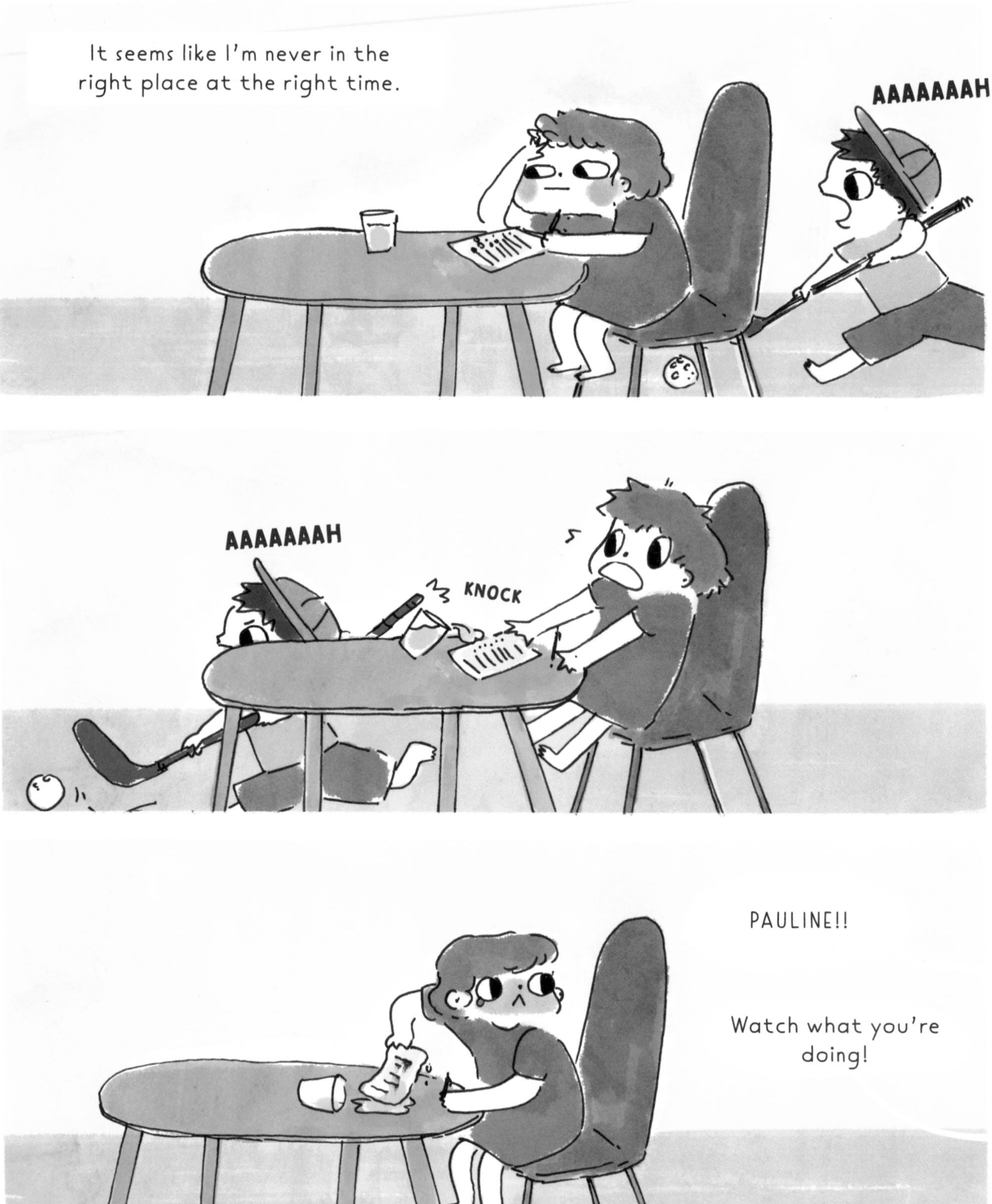
It seems like I'm never in the right place at the right time.
AAAAAAAH
AAAAAAAH
KNOCK
PAULINE!!
Watch what you're doing!

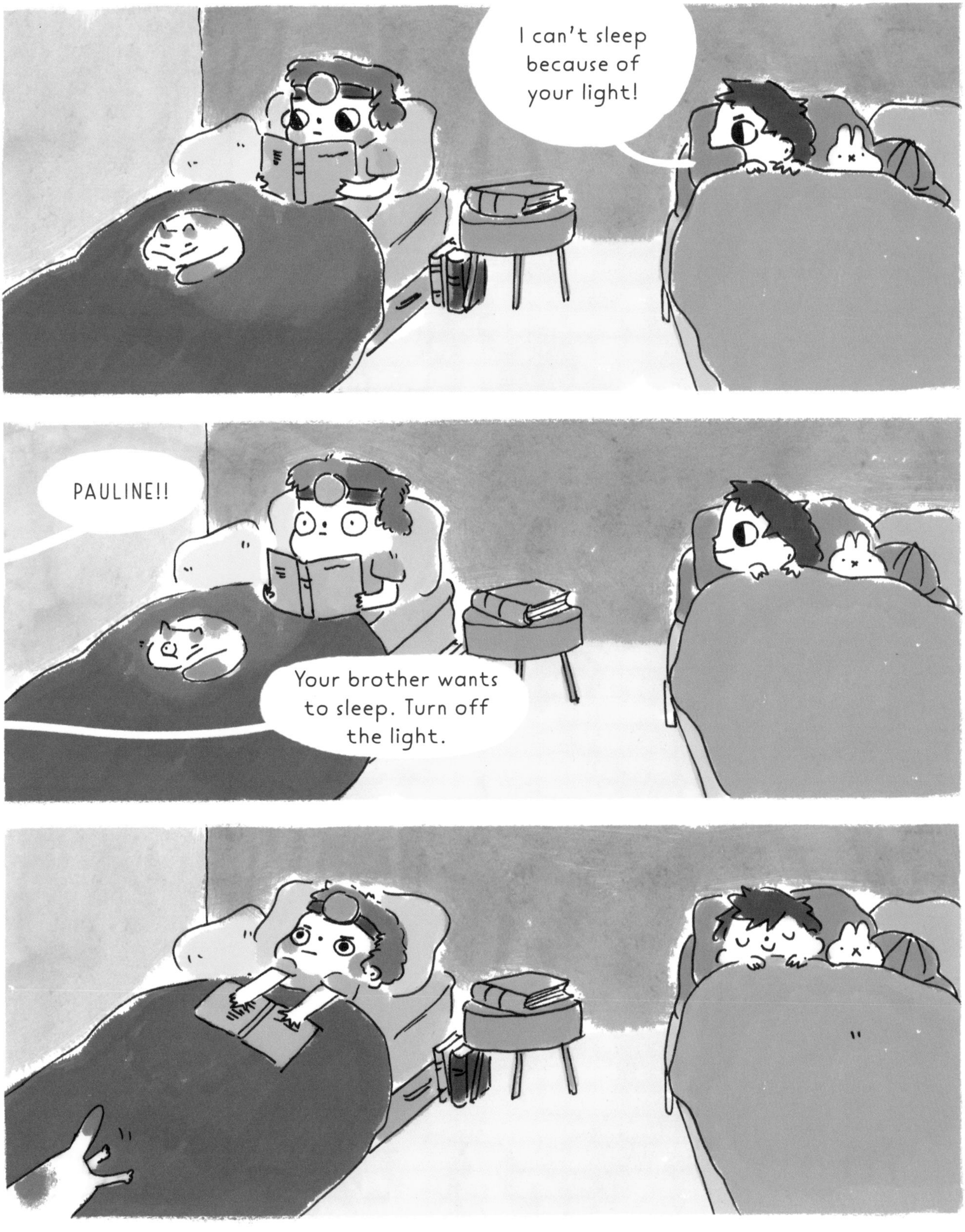
I can't sleep because of your light!
PAULINE!!
Your brother wants to sleep. Turn off the light.

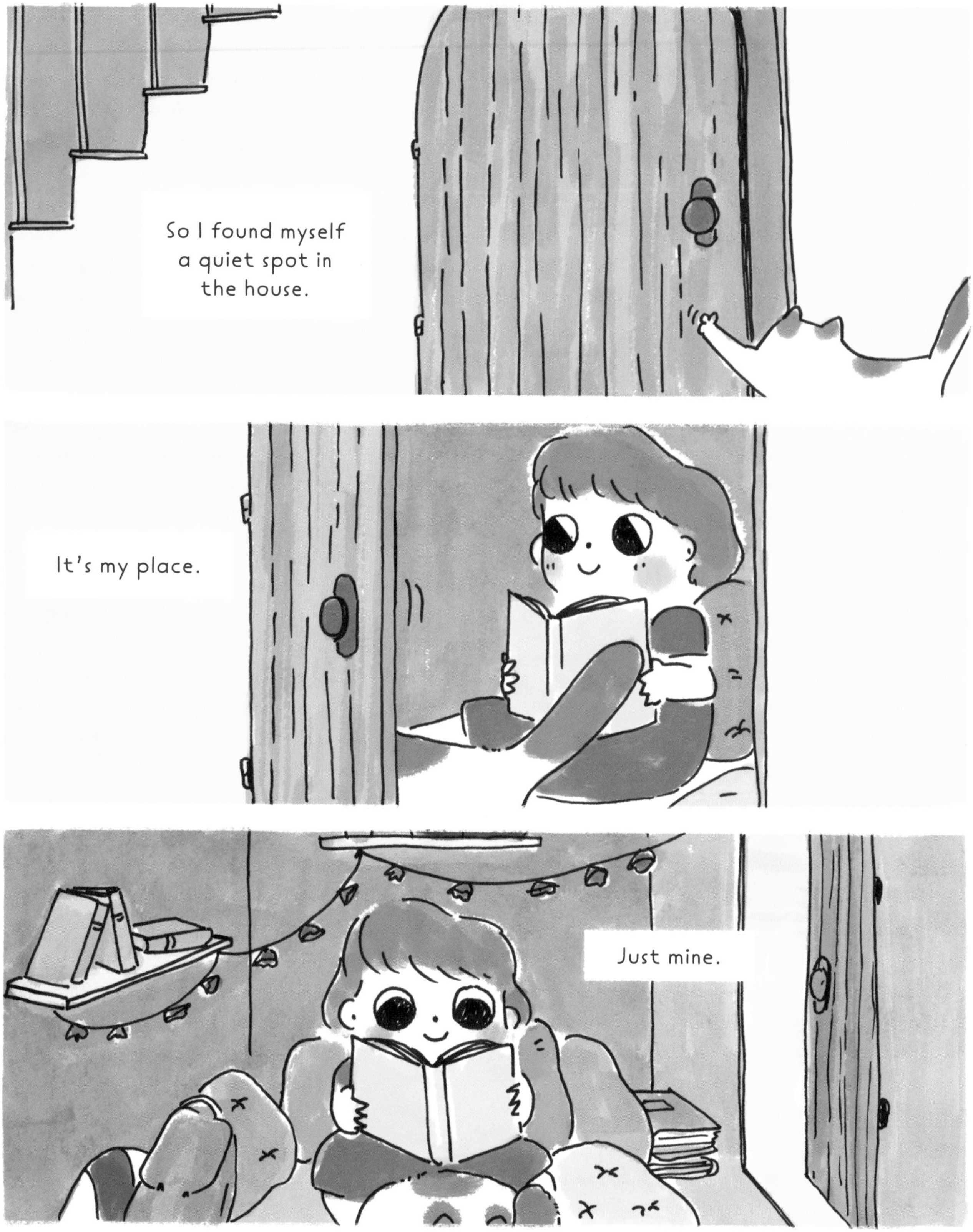
So I found myself a quiet spot in the house.
It's my place.
Just mine.

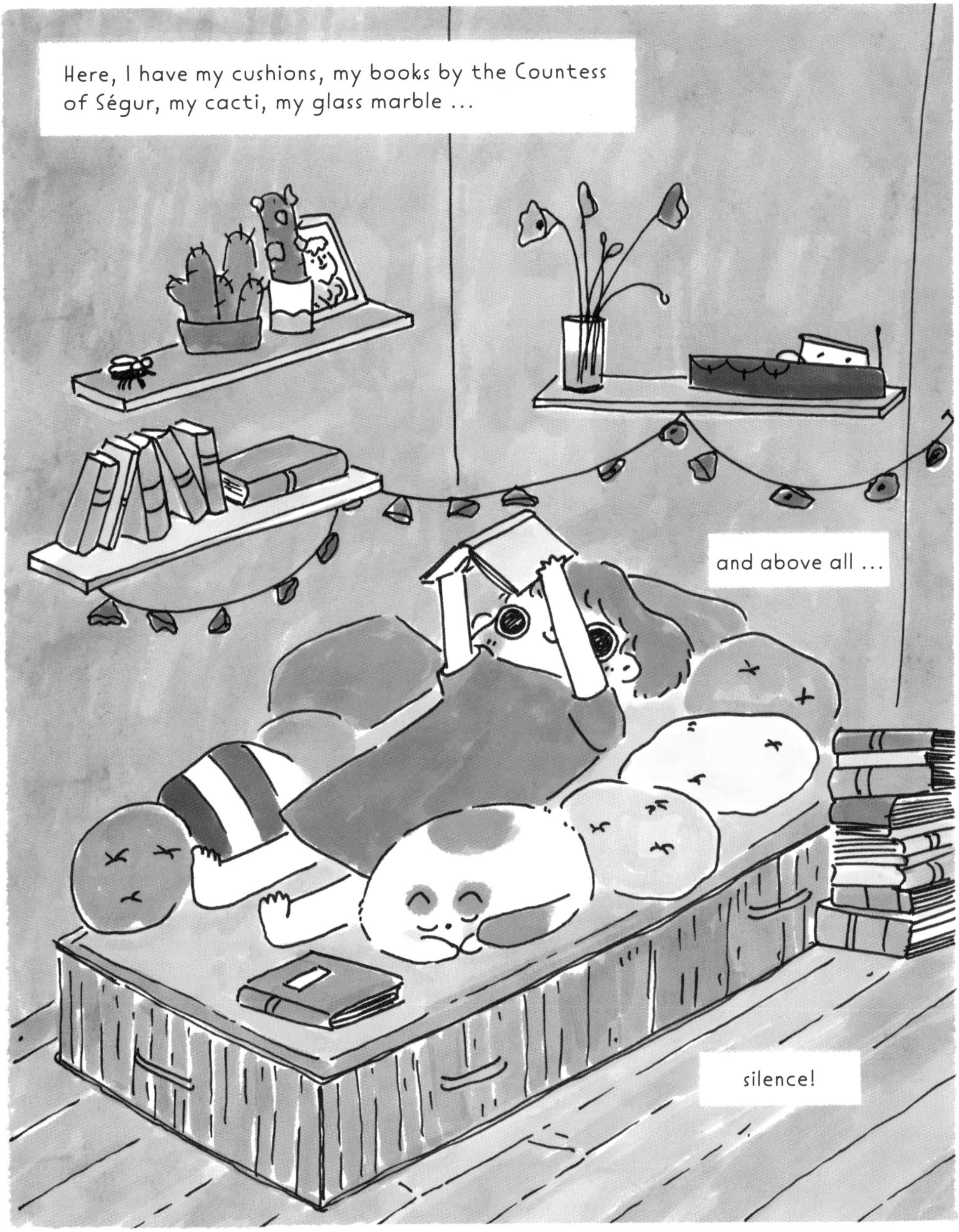
Here, I have my cushions, my books by the Countess of Ségur, my cacti, my glass marble ...
and above all ...
silence!

Here, I am left in peace. Nobody tells me what to do.

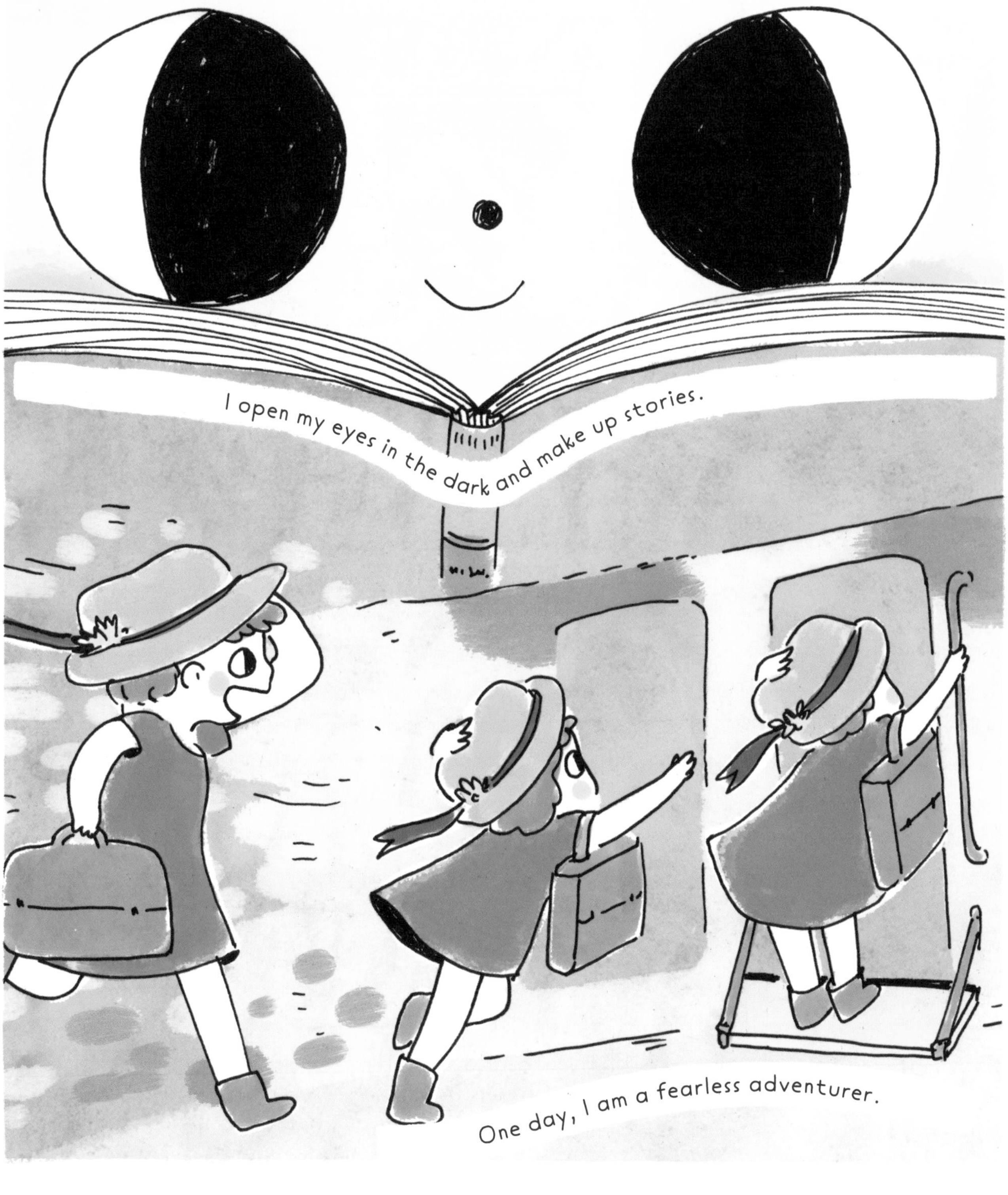
I open my eyes in the dark and make up stories.
One day, I am a fearless adventurer.

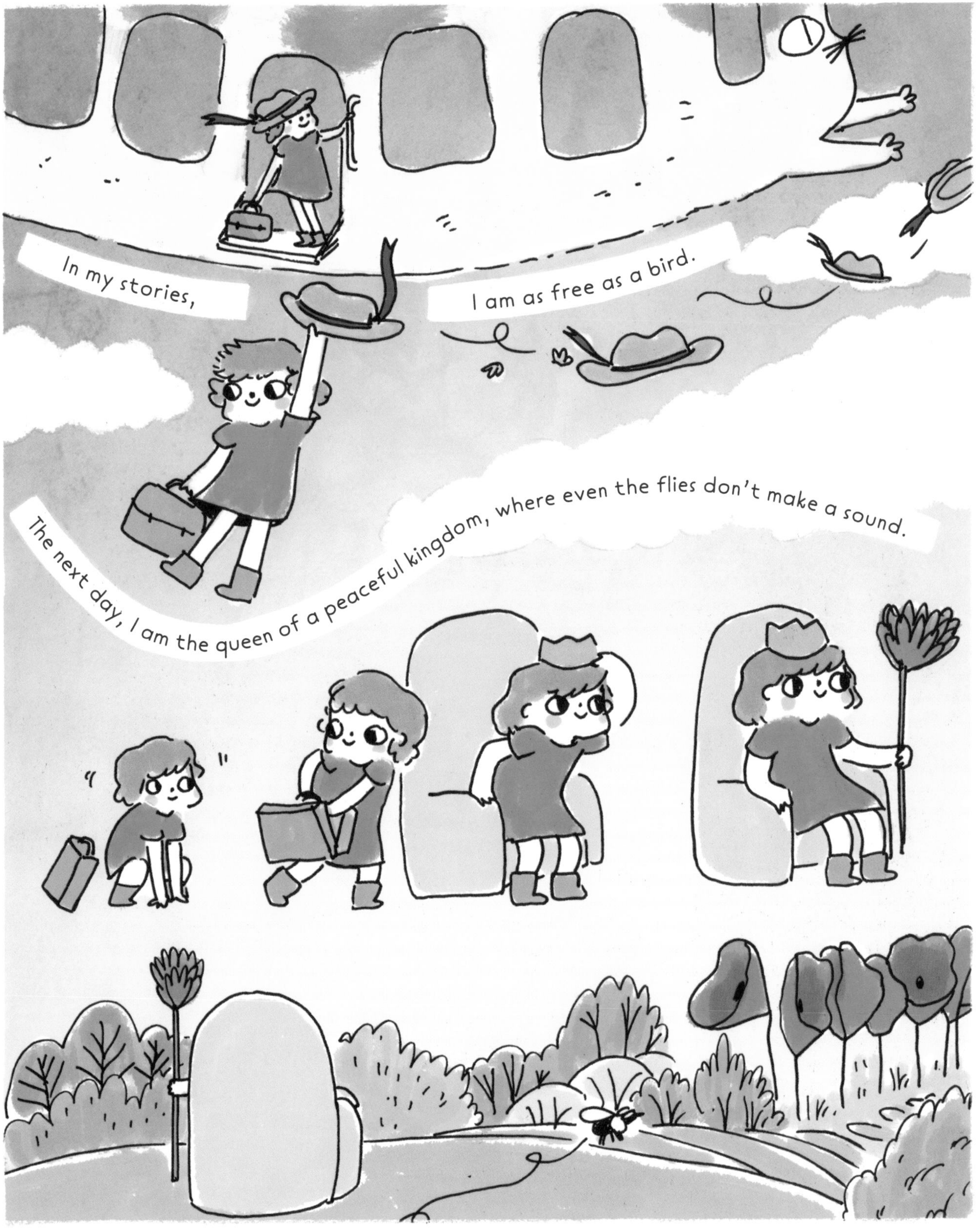
In my stories,
I am as free as a bird.
The next day, I am the queen of a peaceful kingdom, where even the flies don't make a sound.

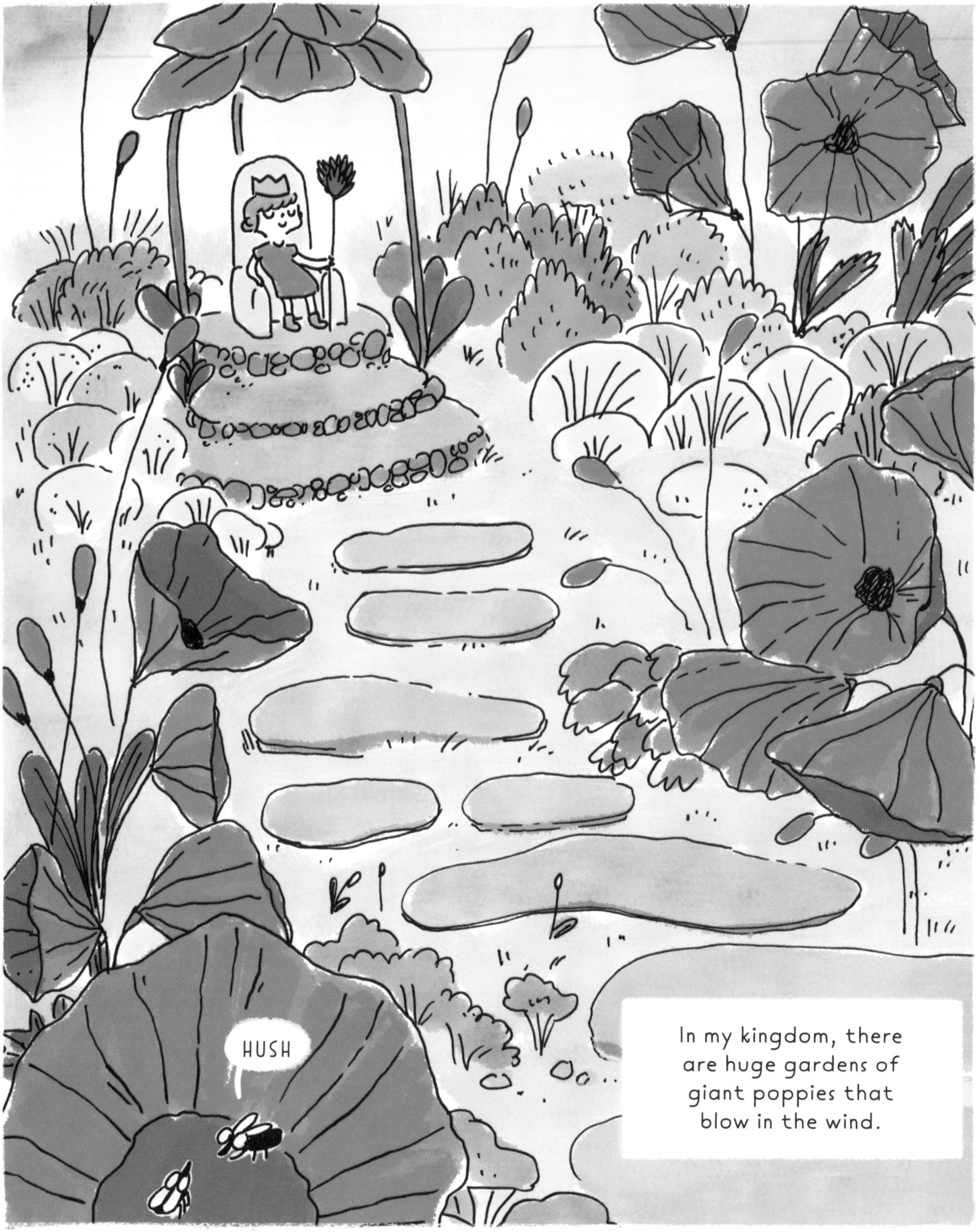
HUSH
In my kingdom, there are huge gardens of giant poppies that blow in the wind.

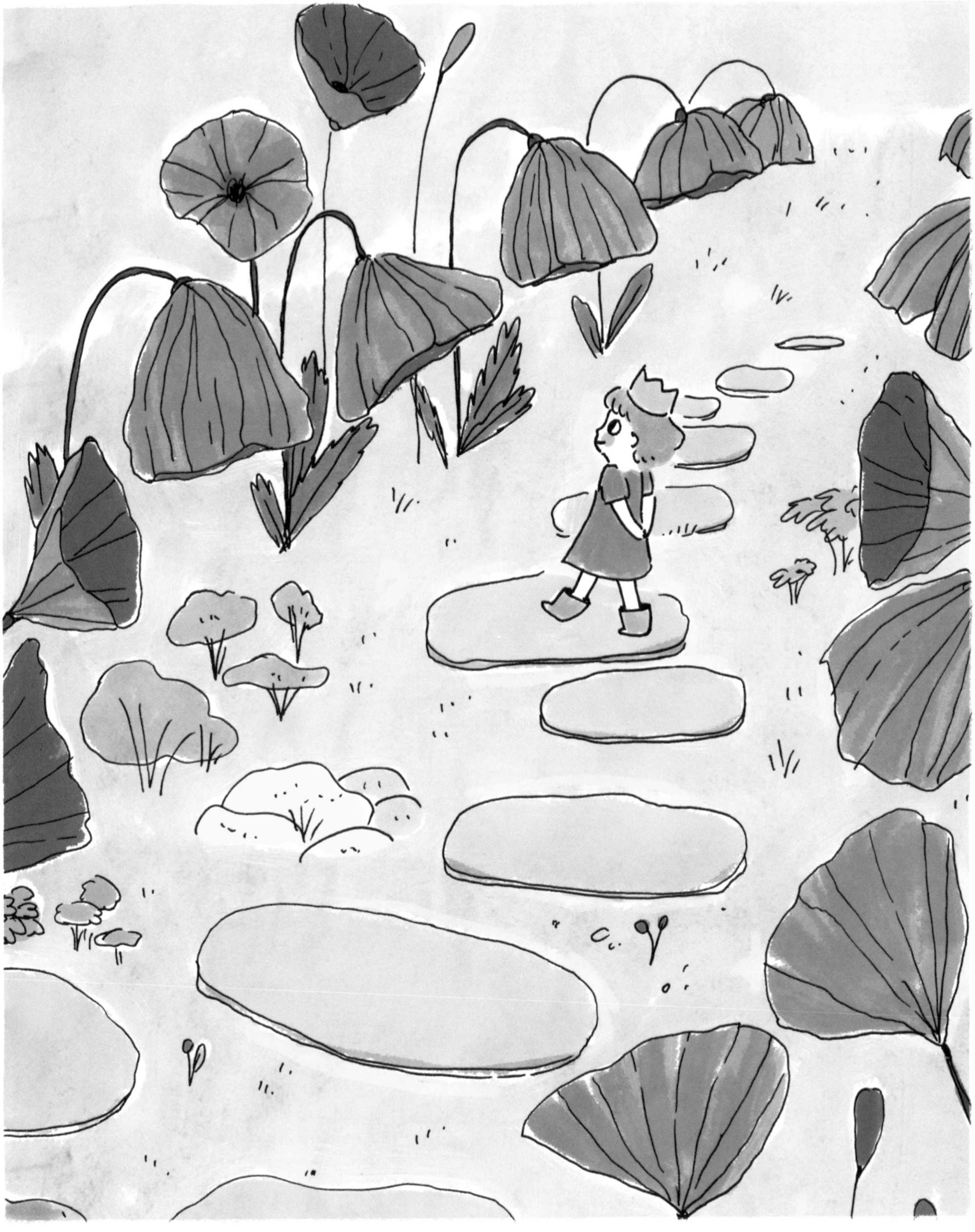

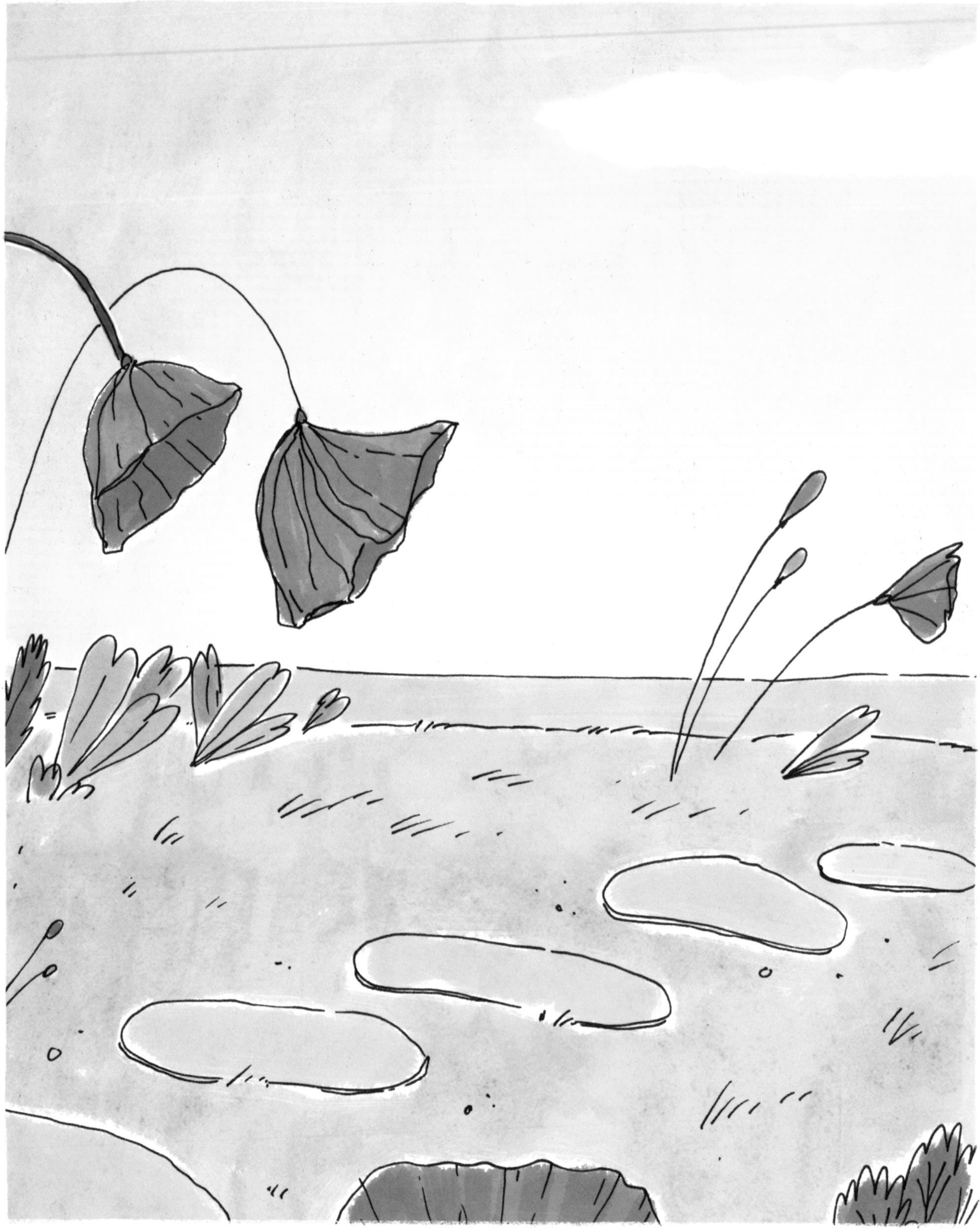

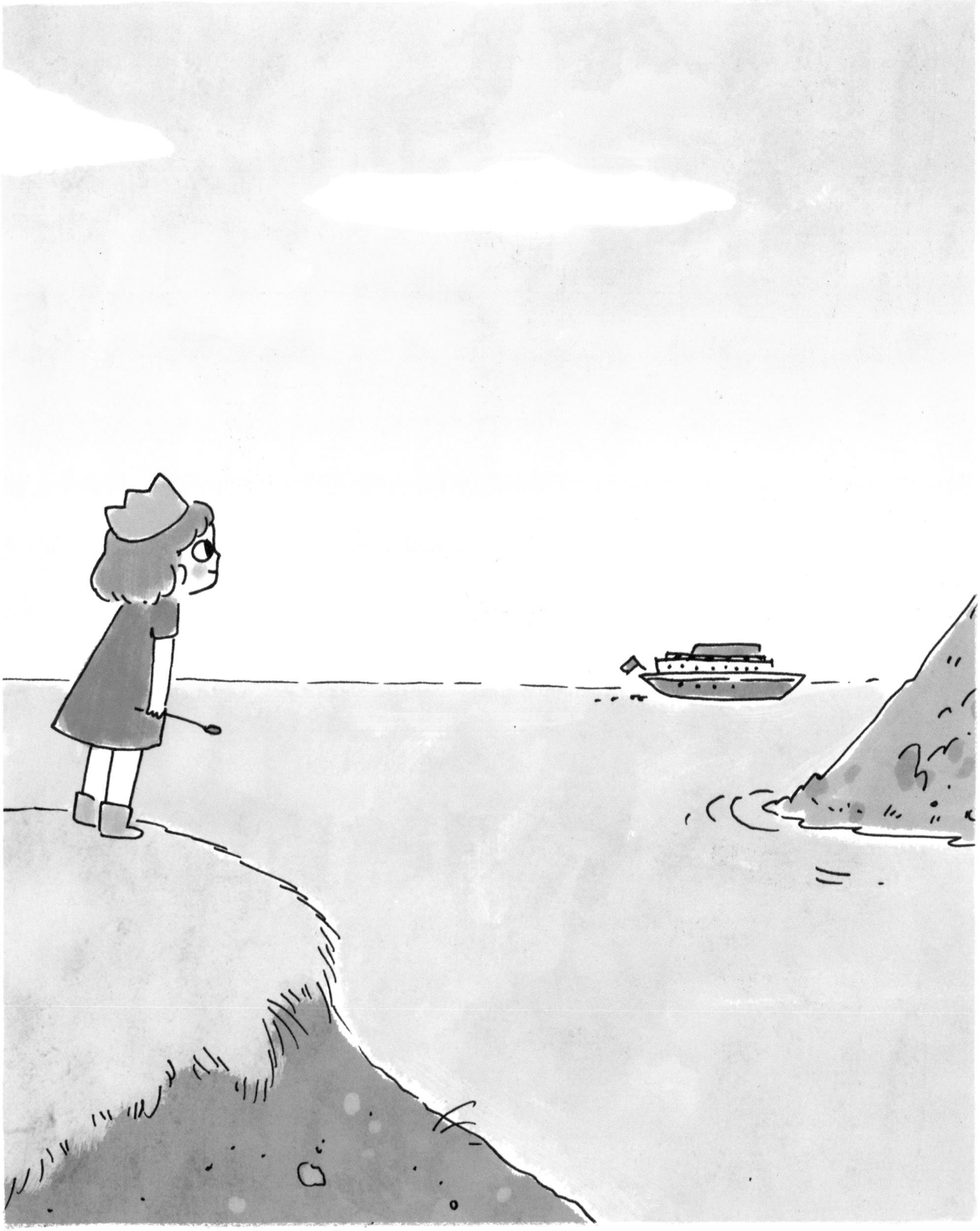

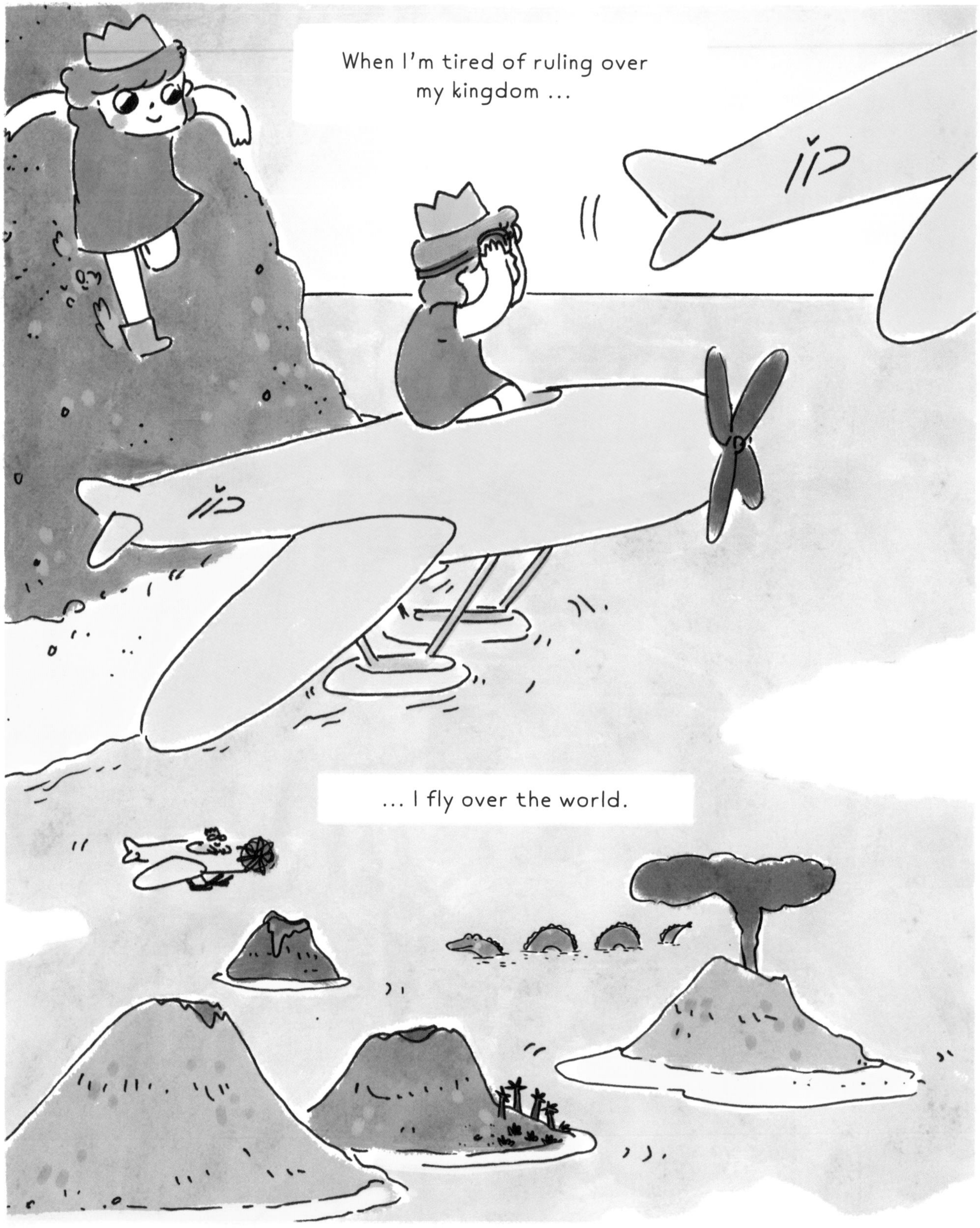
When I'm tired of ruling over my kingdom ...
... I fly over the world.

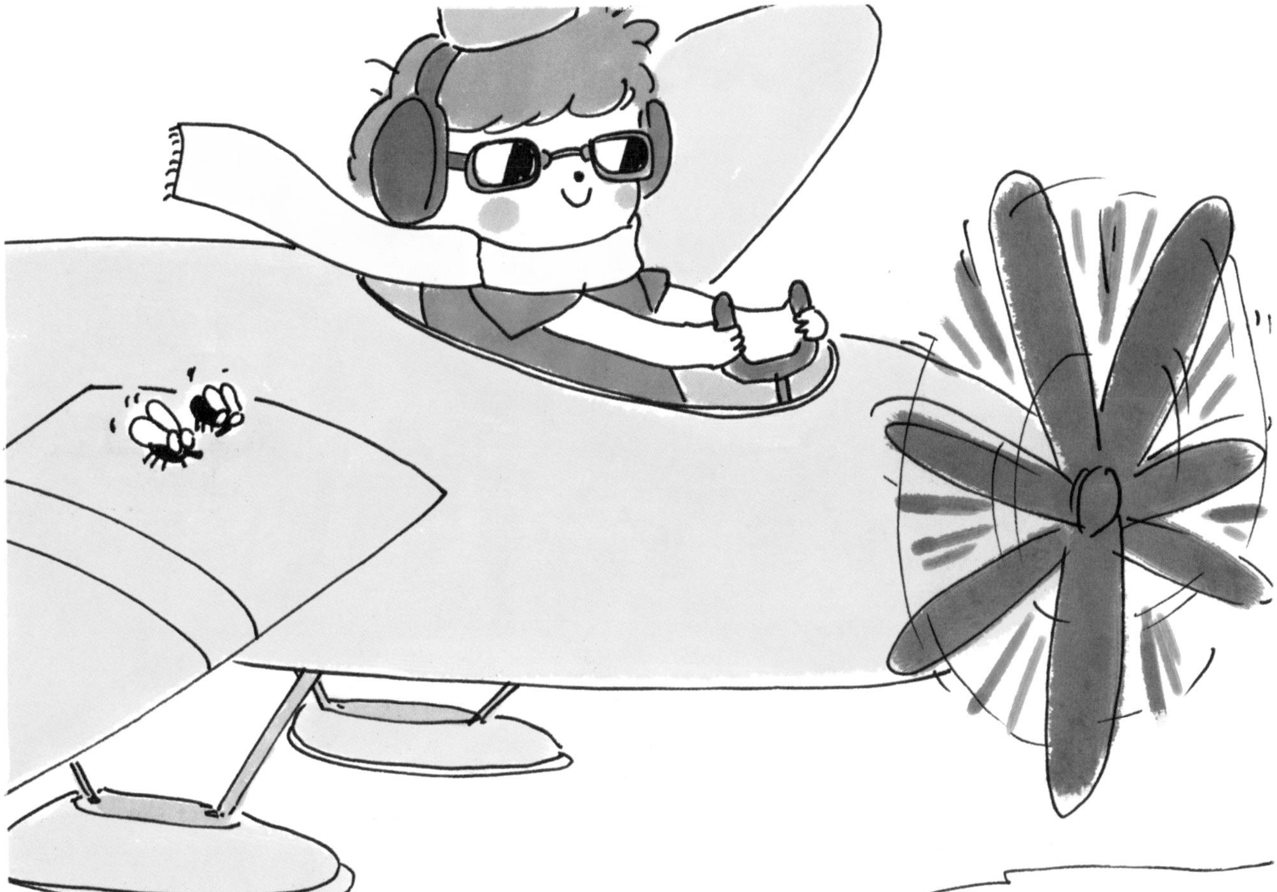

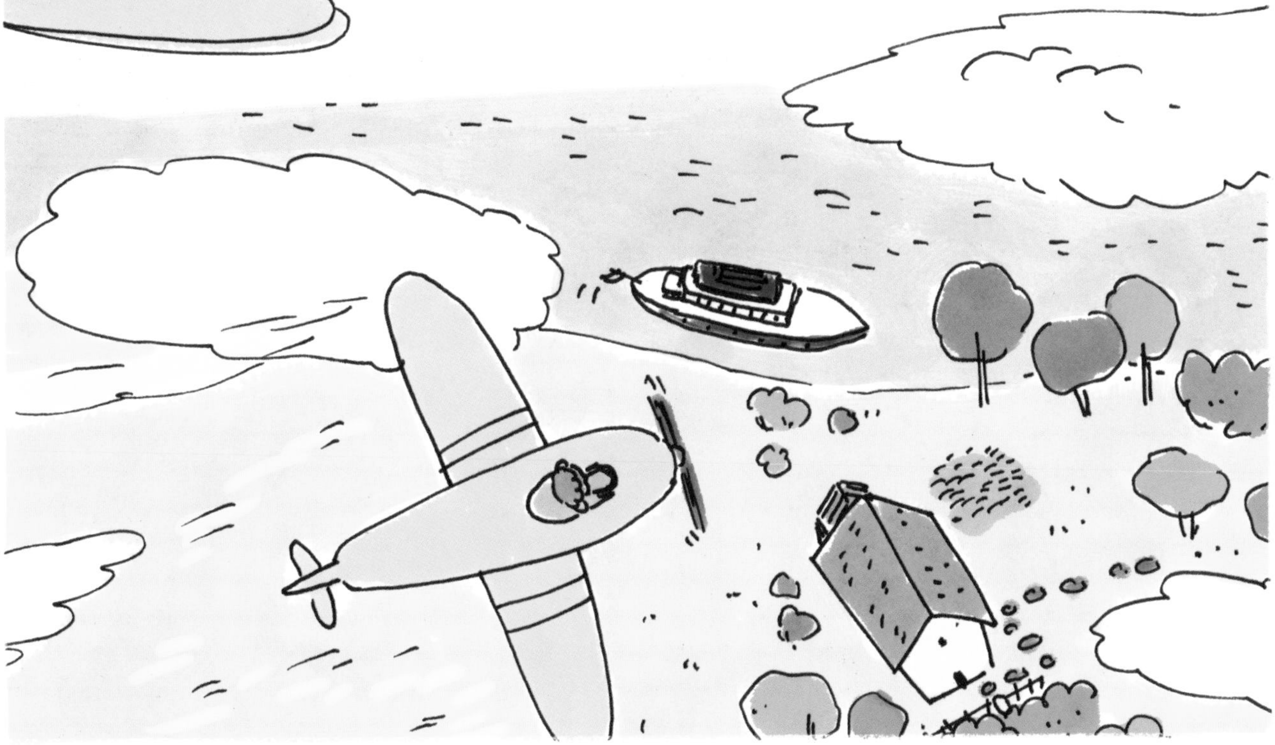

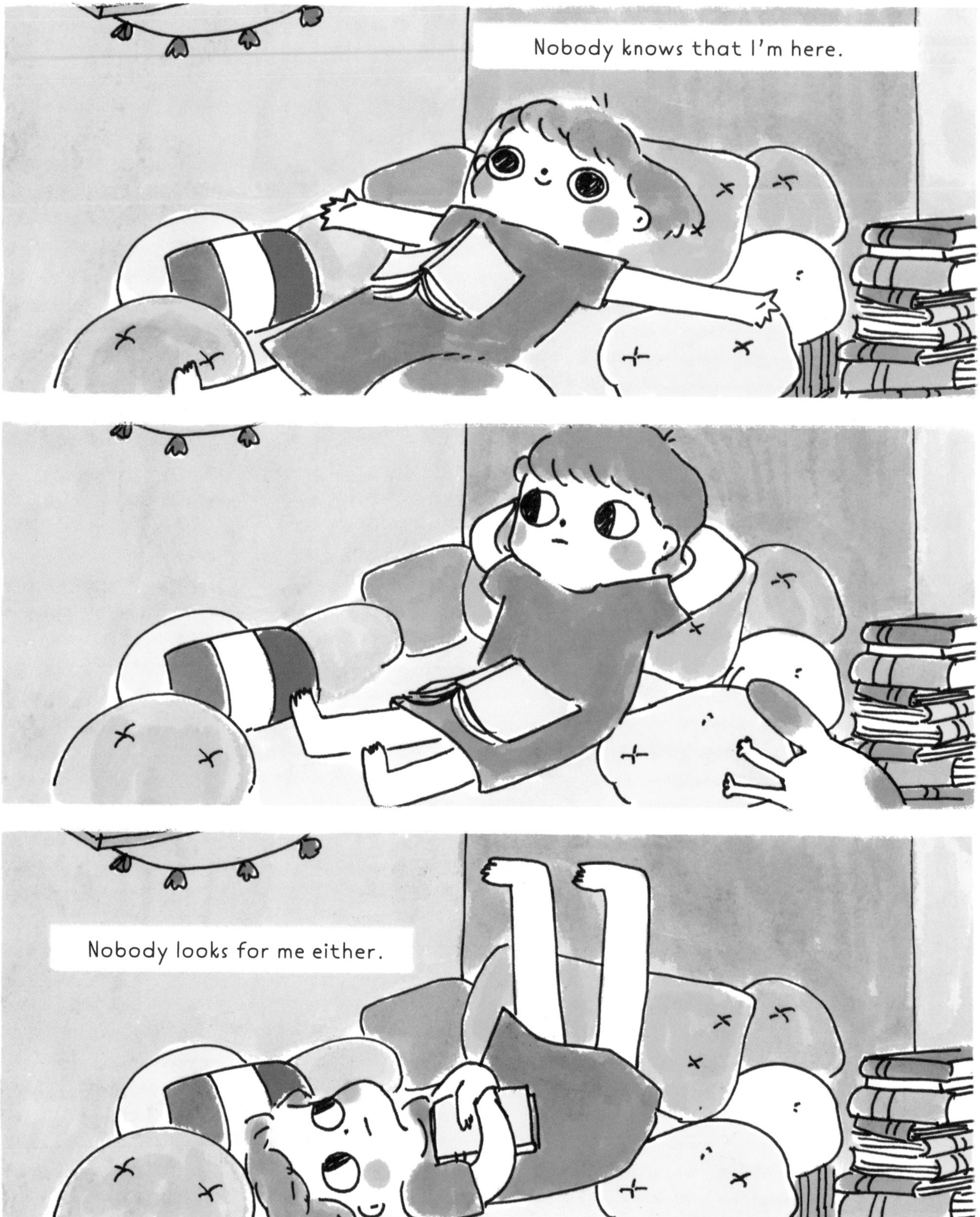
Nobody knows that I'm here.
Nobody looks for me either.

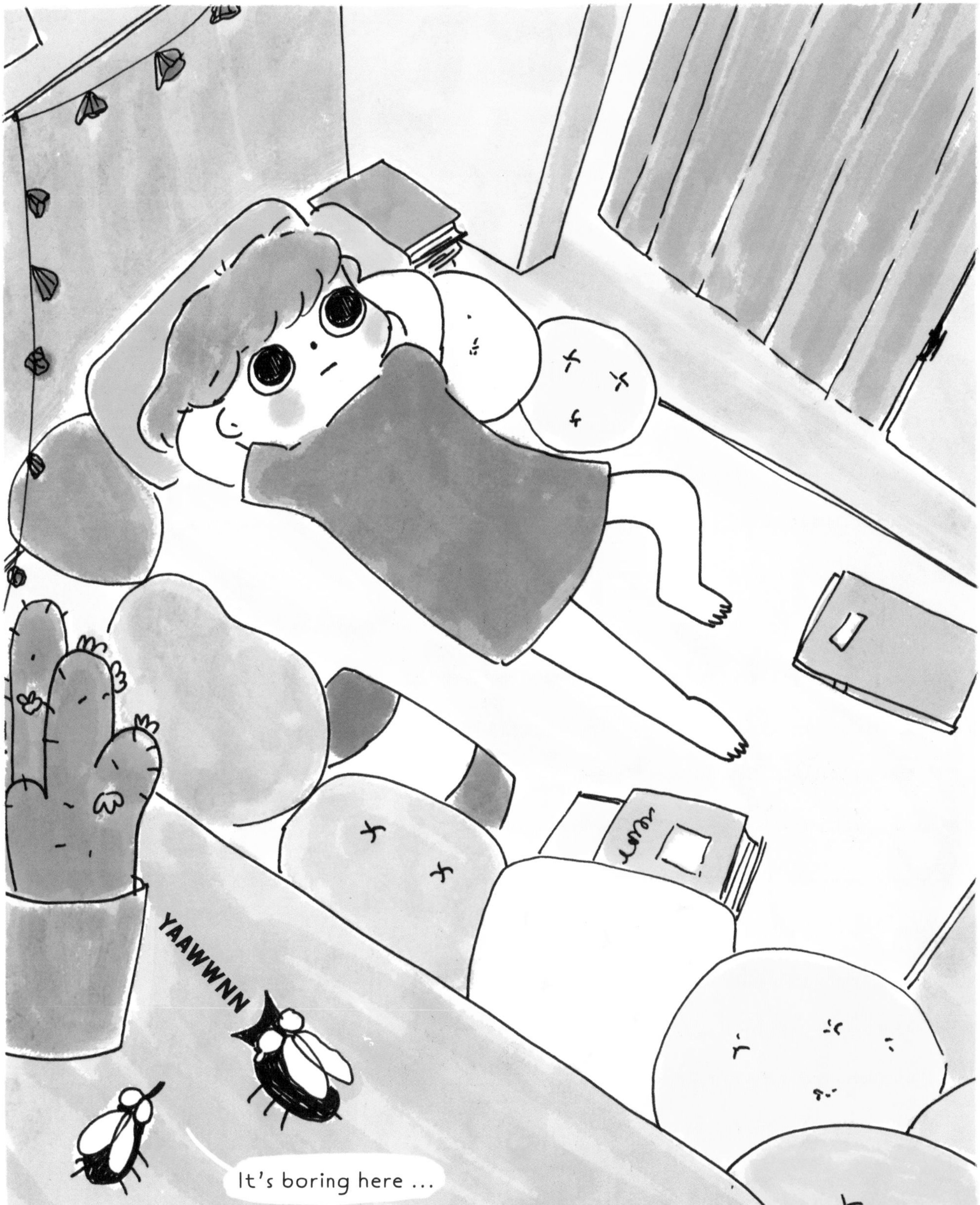
YAAWWNN
It's boring here ...

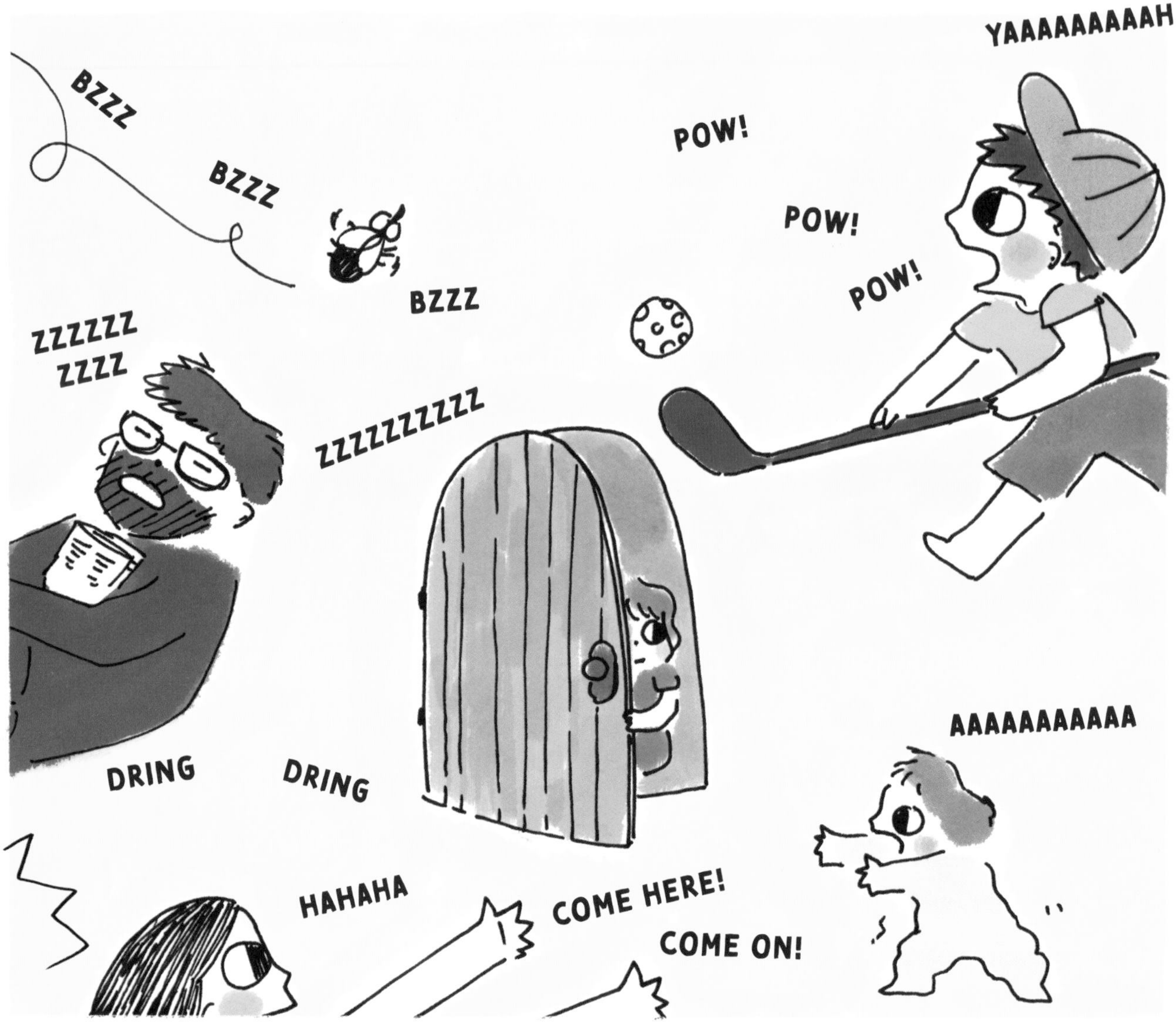
BZZZ
BZZZ
BZZZ
POW!
POW!
POW!
YAAAAAAAAAH
ZZZZZZ
ZZZZ
ZZZZZZZZZZ
DRING
DRING
AAAAAAAAAAA
HAHAHA
COME HERE!
COME ON!

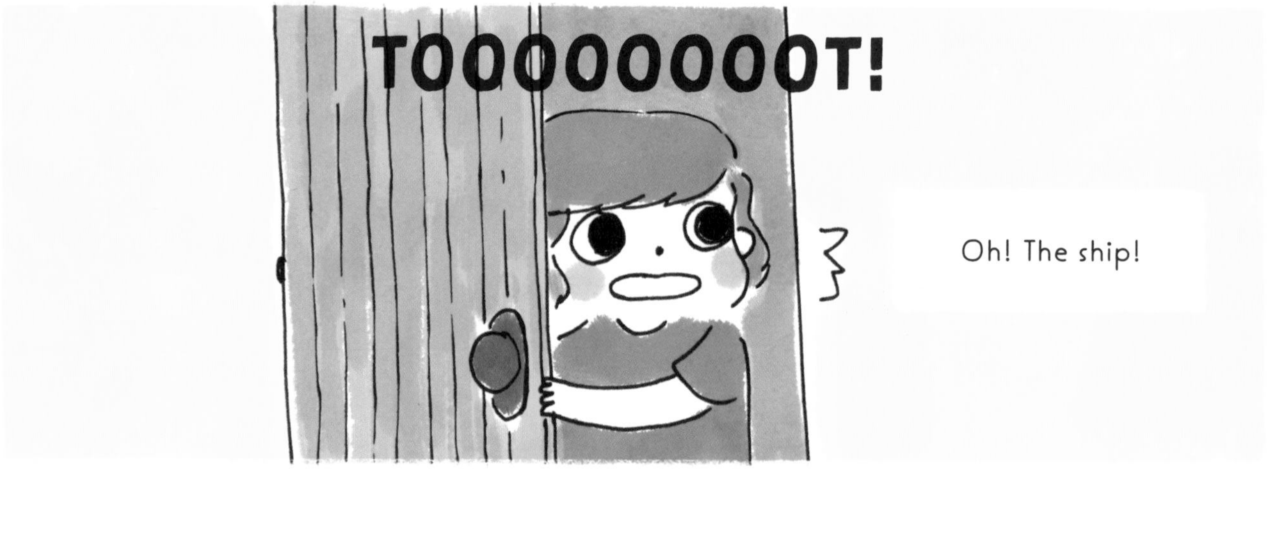
TOOOOOOOOT!
Oh! The ship!

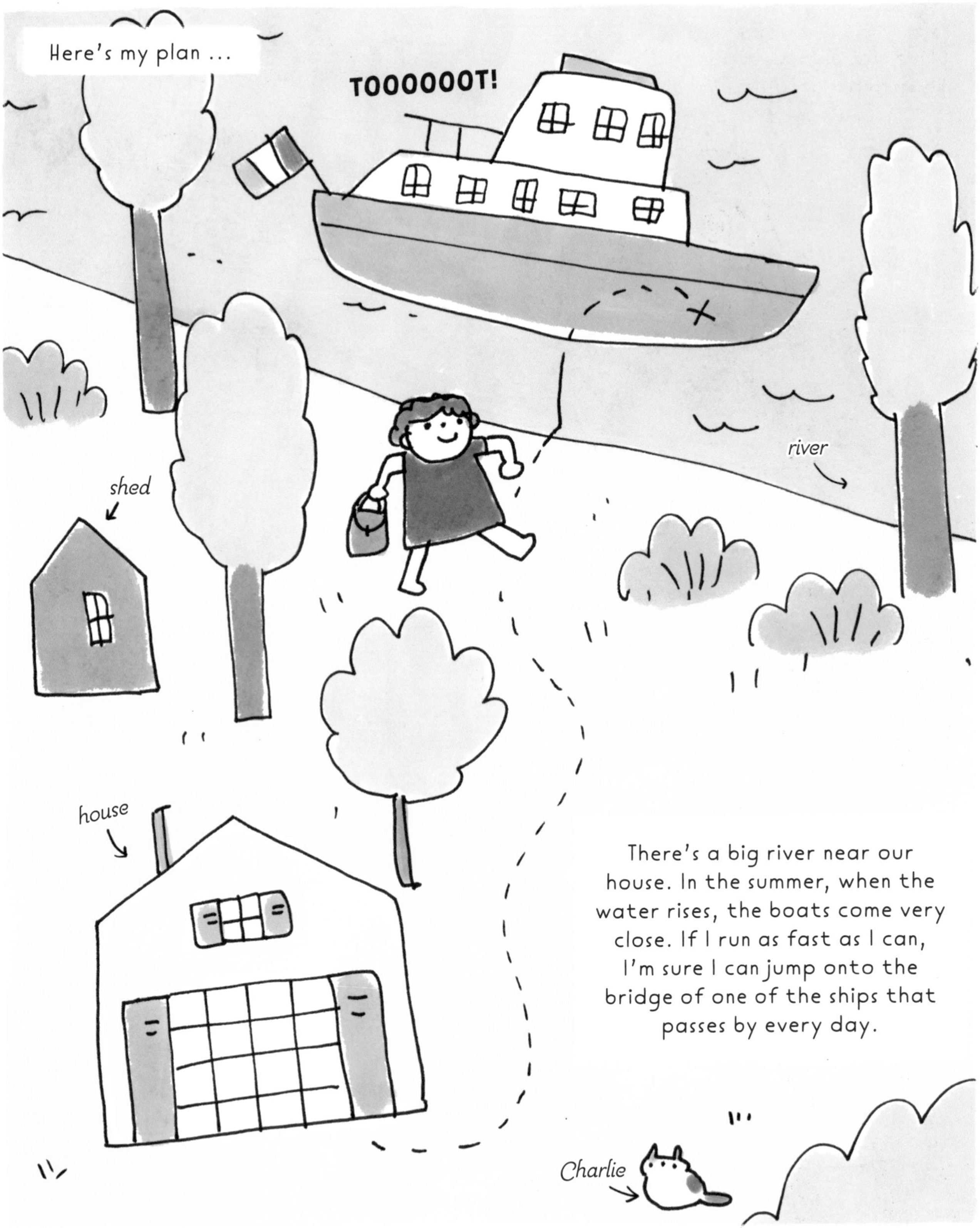
Here's my plan ...
TOOOOOOT!
shed
river
house
Charlie

There's a big river near our house. In the summer, when the water rises, the boats come very close. If I run as fast as I can, I'm sure I can jump onto the bridge of one of the ships that passes by every day.

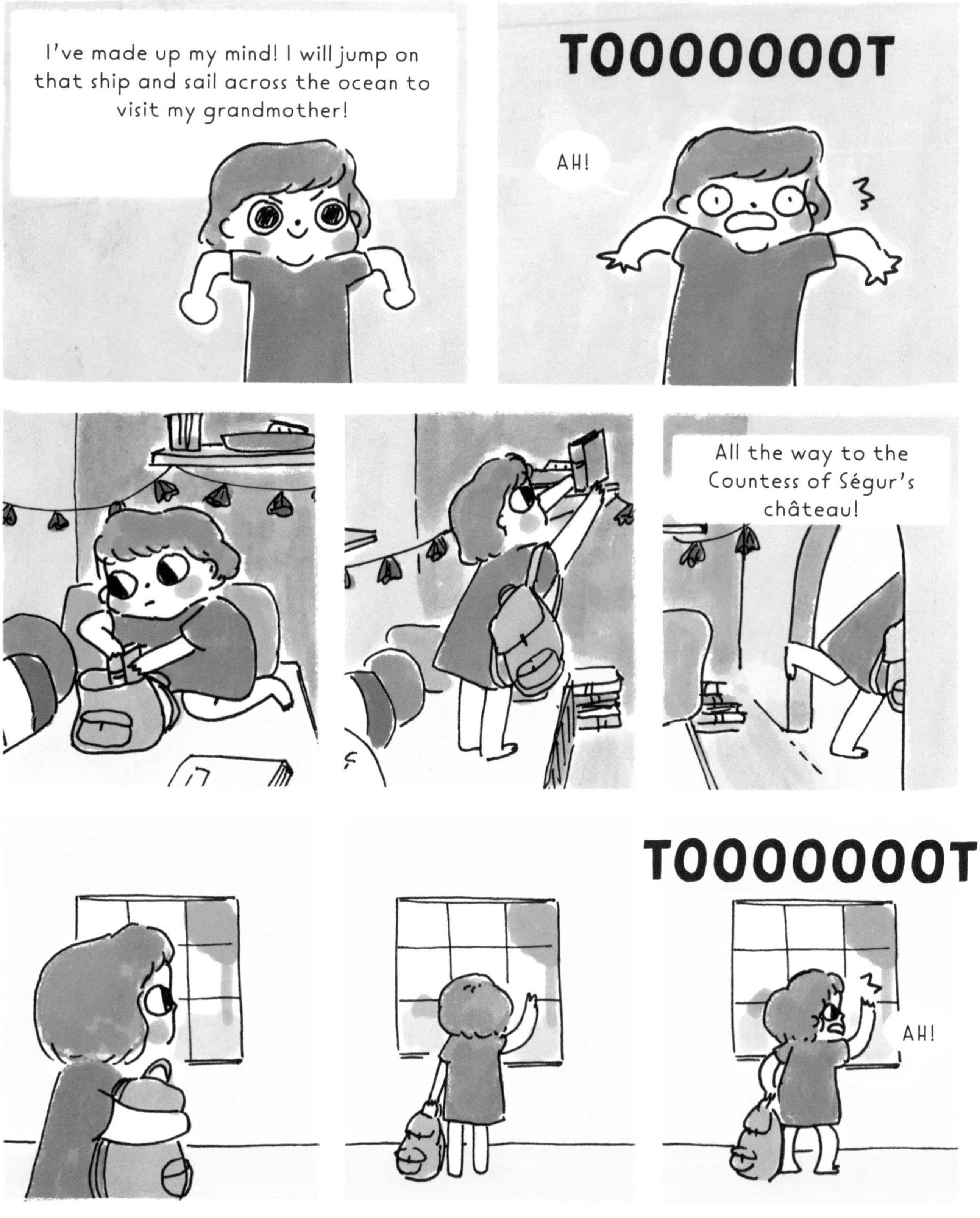
I've made up my mind! I will jump on that ship and sail across the ocean to visit my grandmother!
TOOOOOOOT
AH!
All the way to the Countess of Ségur's château!
TOOOOOOOT
AH!

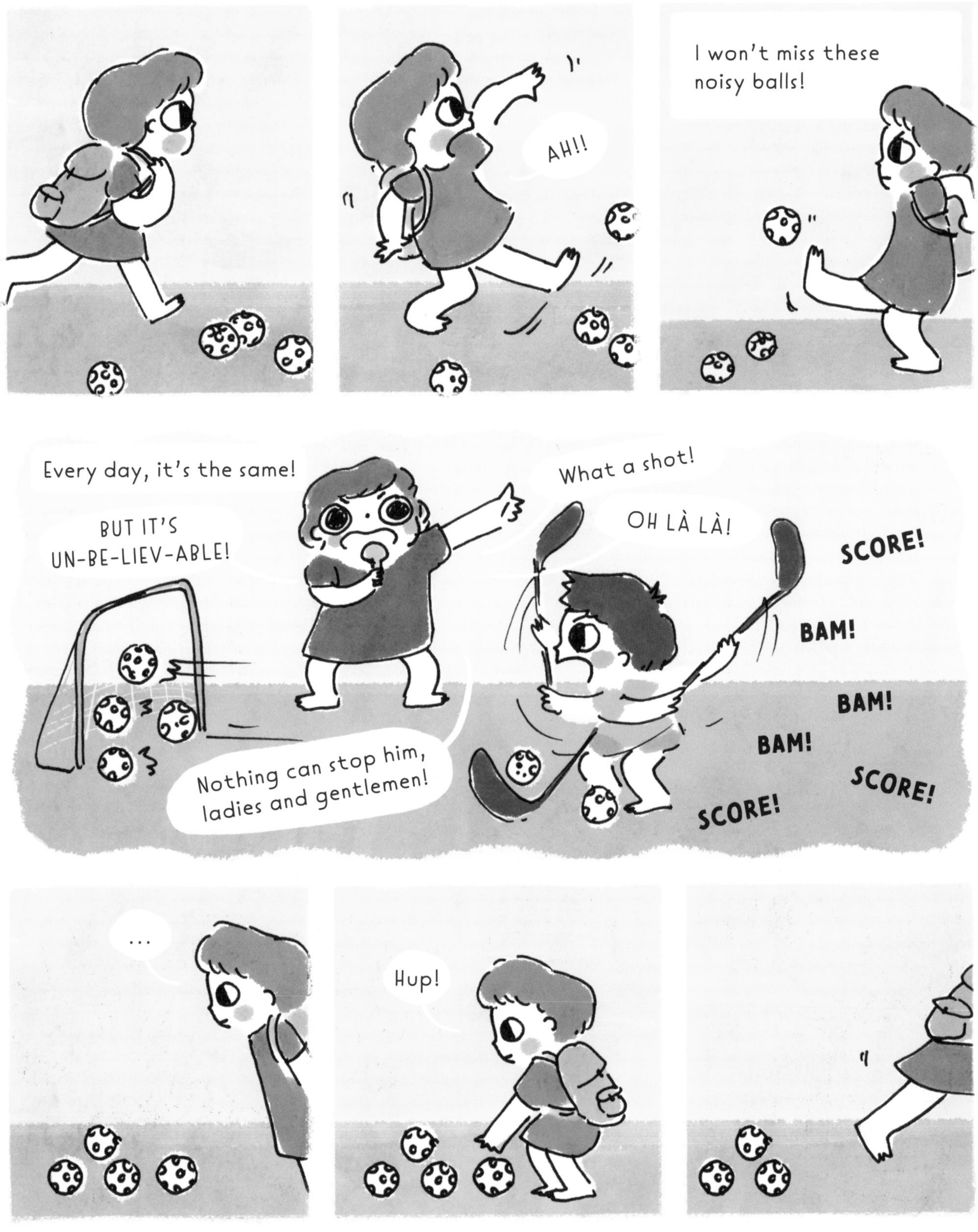
AH!!
I won't miss these noisy balls!
Every day, it's the same!
BUT IT'S UN-BE-LIEV-ABLE!
What a shot!
OH LÀ LÀ!
Nothing can stop him, ladies and gentlemen!
SCORE!
BAM!
BAM!
BAM!
SCORE!
SCORE!
...
Hup!

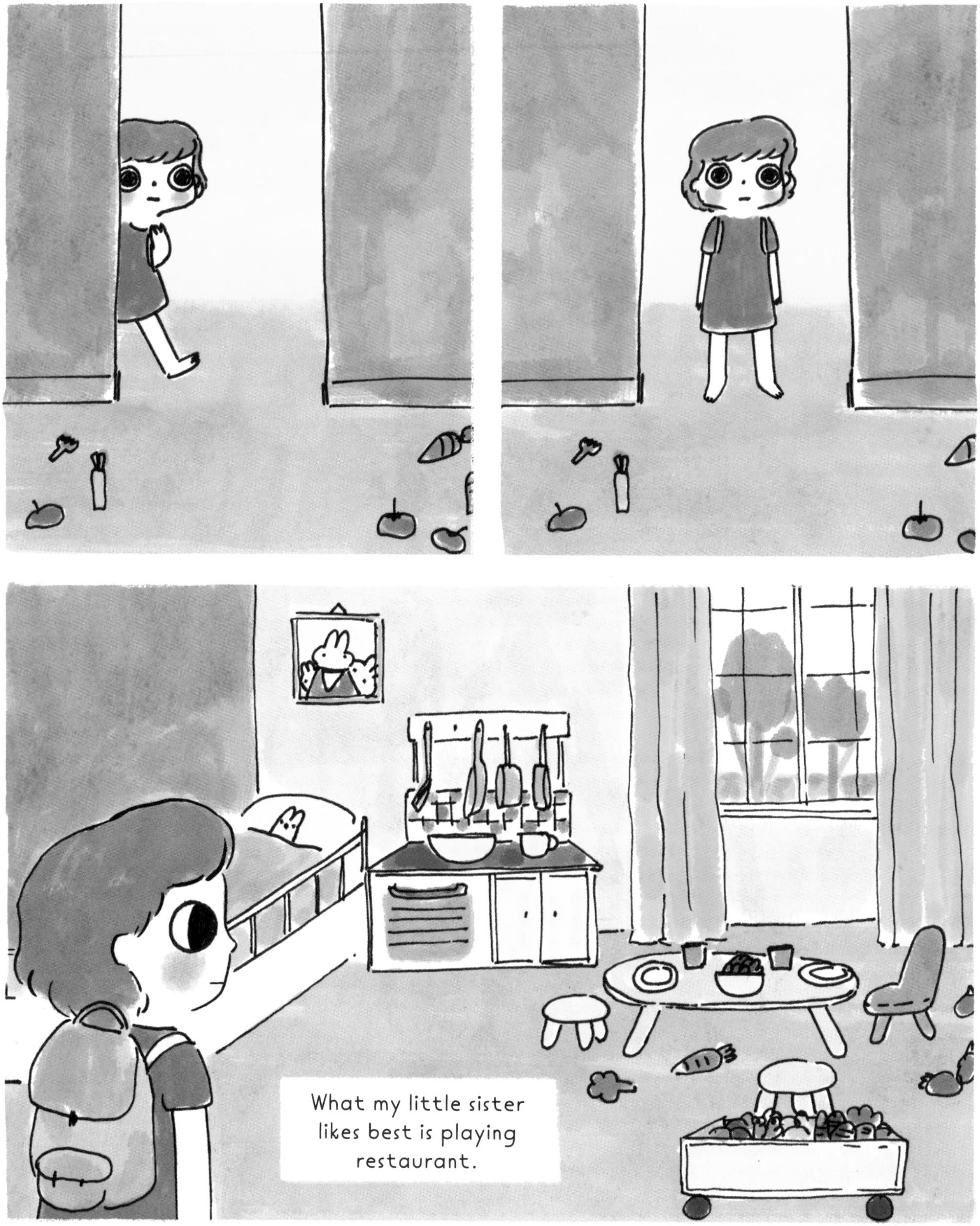
What my little sister likes best is playing restaurant.

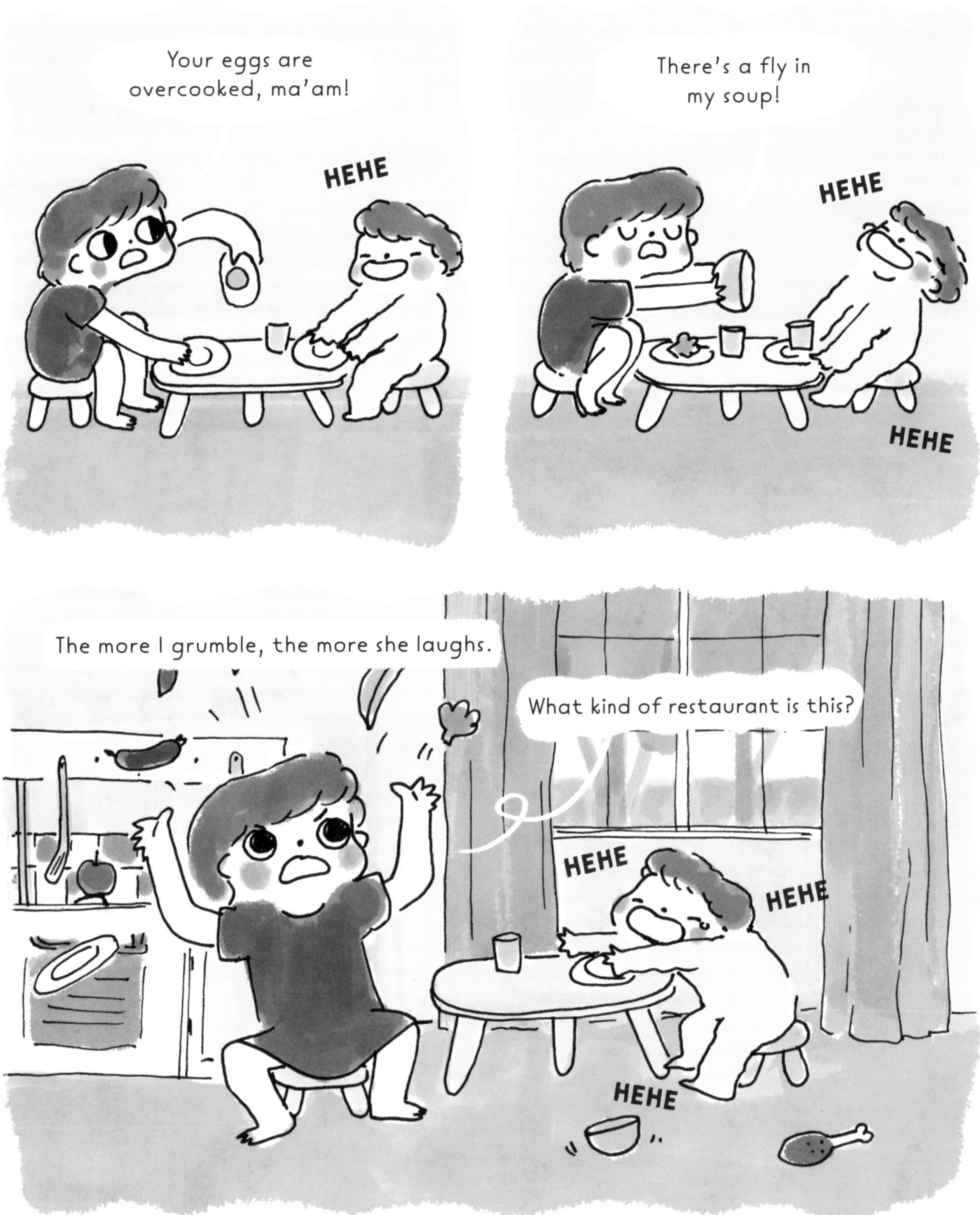
Your eggs are overcooked, ma'am!
HEHE
There's a fly in my soup!
HEHE
HEHE
The more I grumble, the more she laughs.
What kind of restaurant is this?
HEHE
HEHE
HEHE

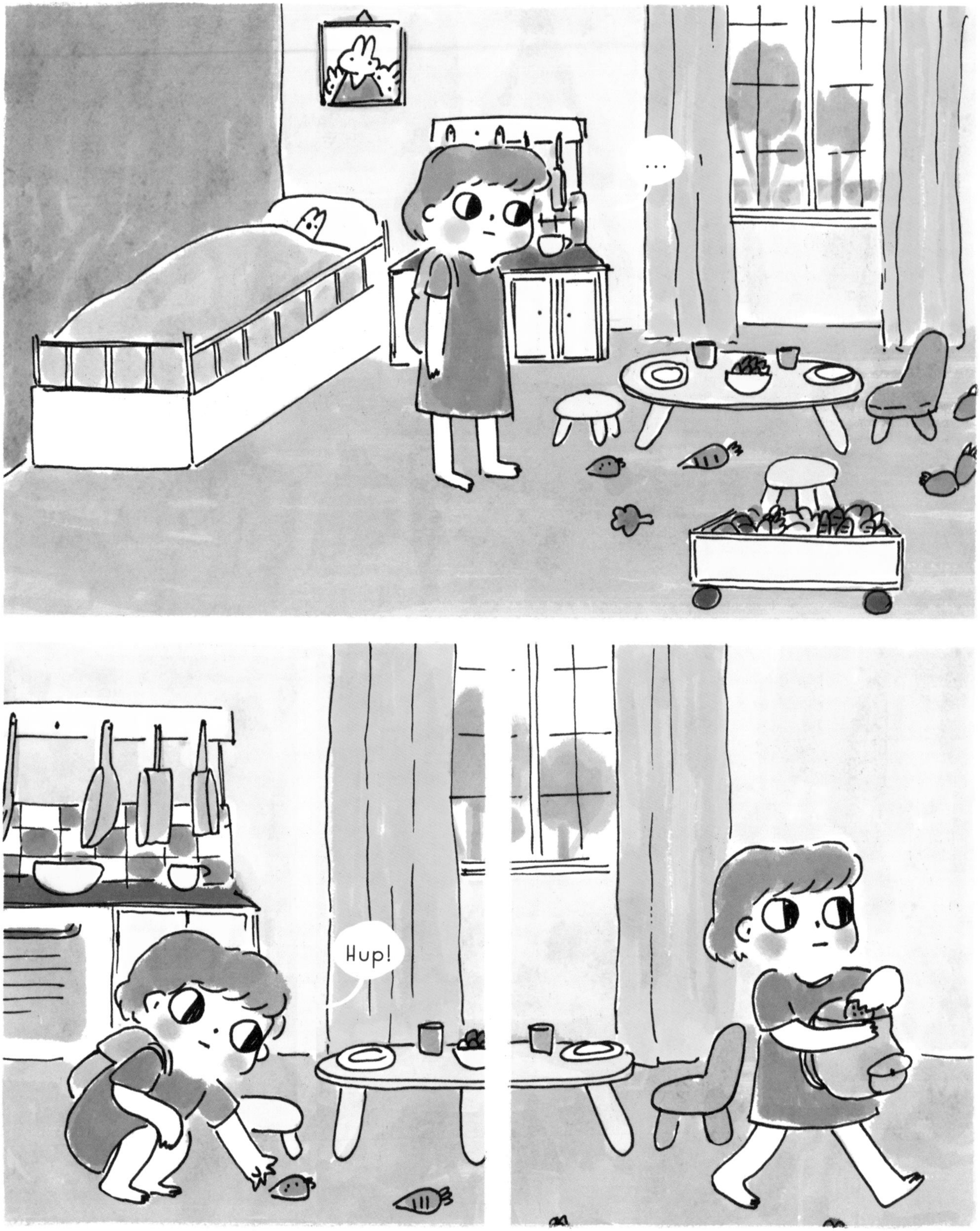
...
Hup!

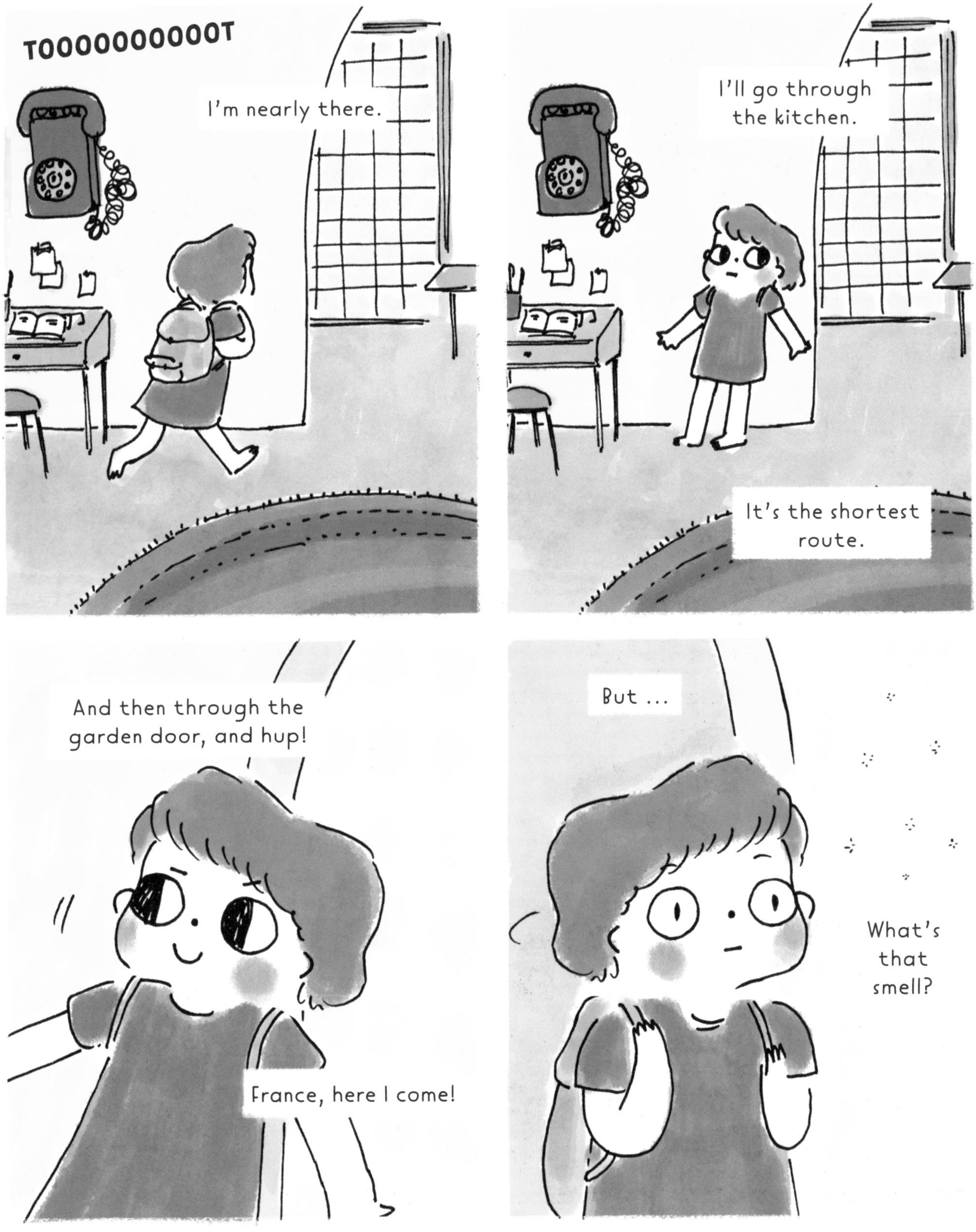
TOOOOOOOOOOT
I'm nearly there.
I'll go through the kitchen.
It's the shortest route.
And then through the garden door, and hup!
France, here I come!
But ...
What's that smell?

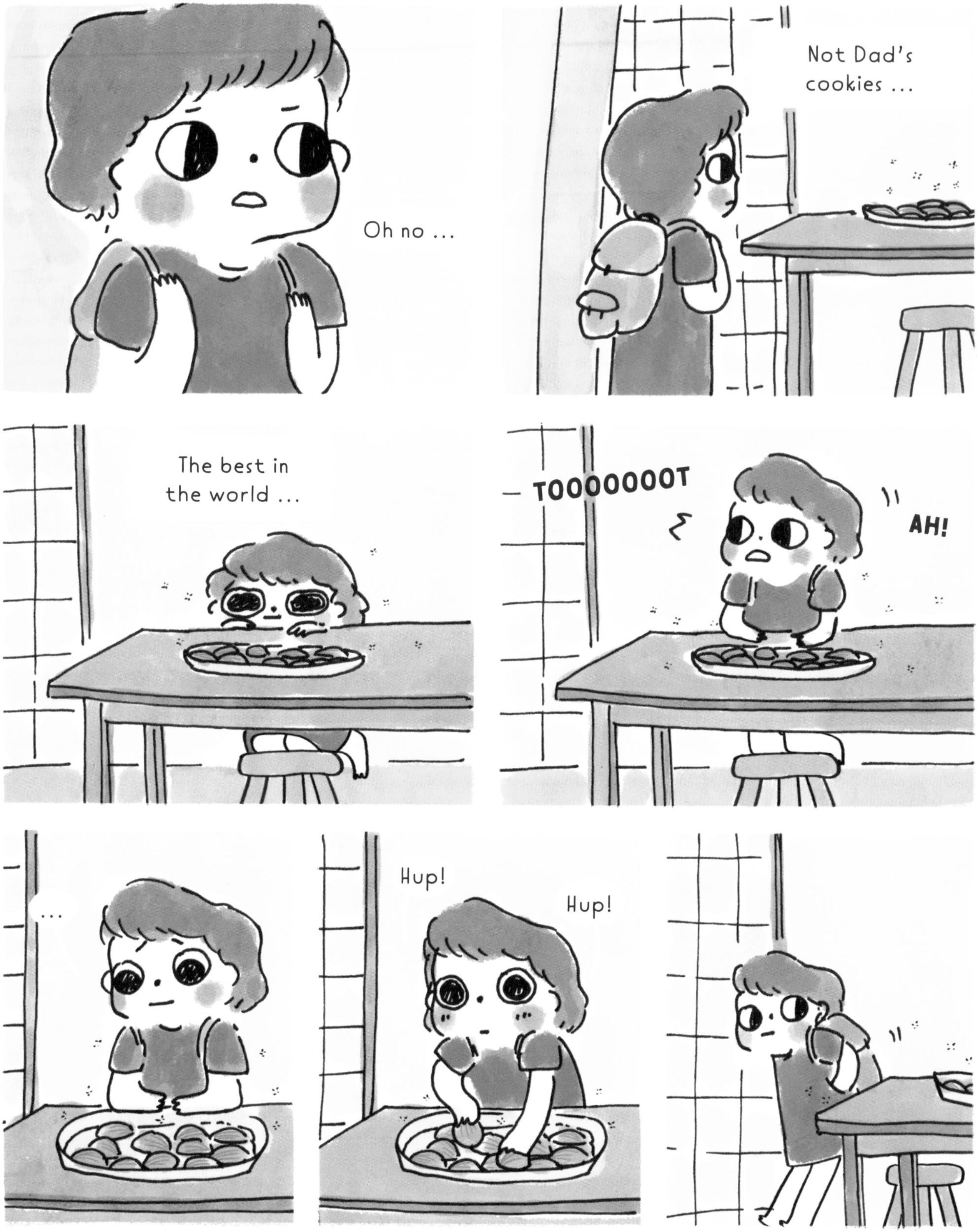

Oh no ...
Not Dad's cookies ...
The best in the world ...
TOOOOOOOT
AH!
...
Hup!
Hup!

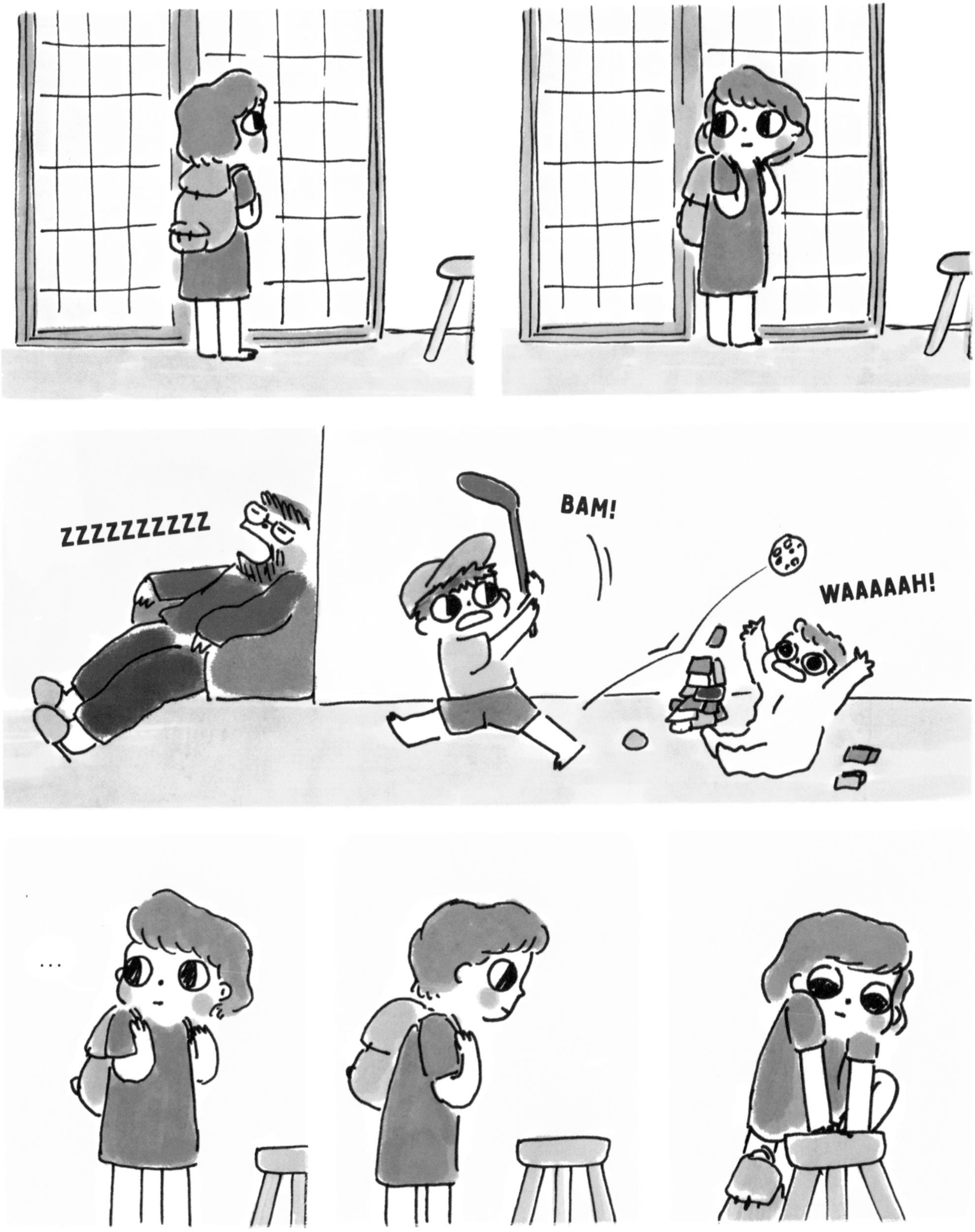
ZZZZZZZZZZ
BAM!
WAAAAAH!
...

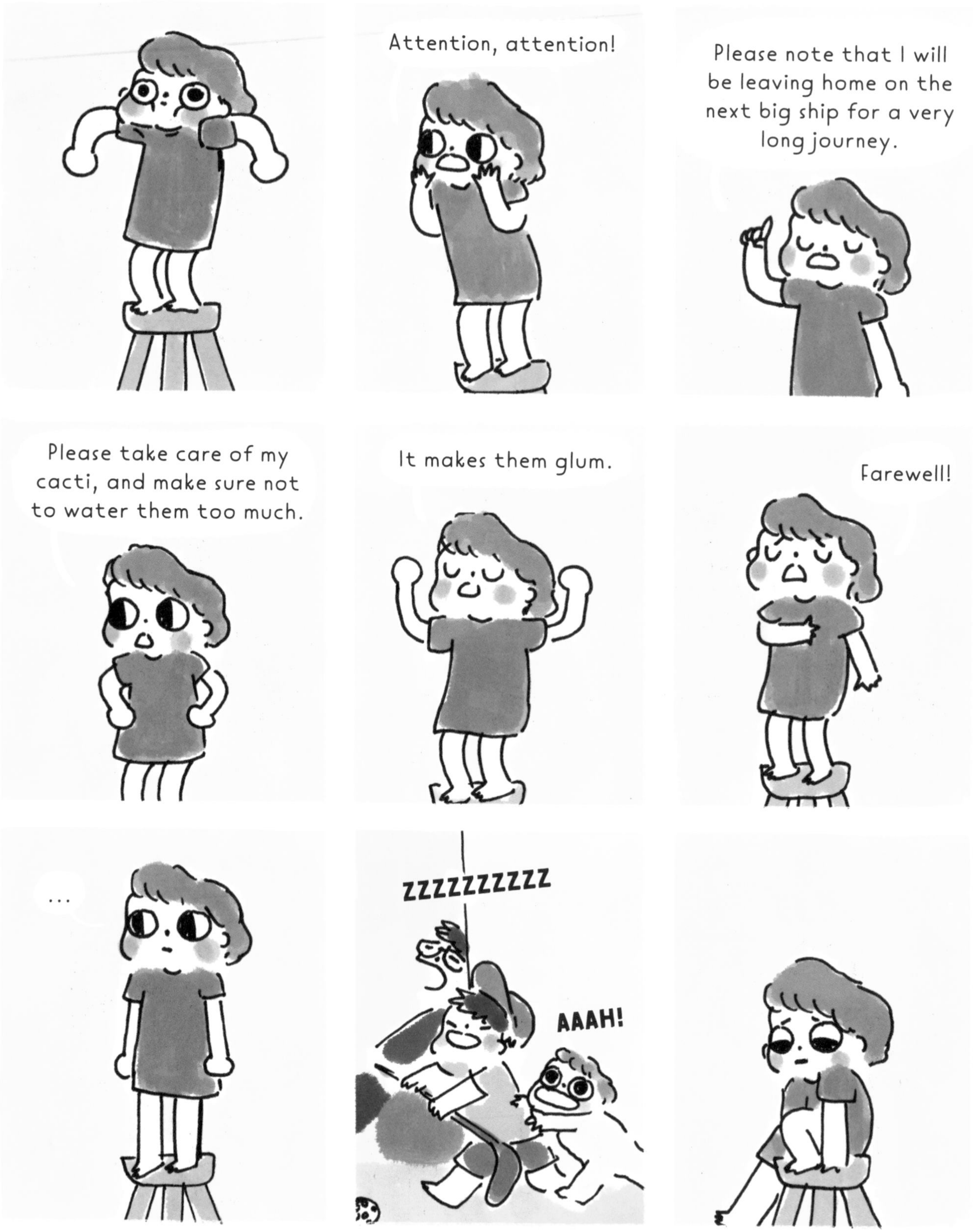
Attention, attention!
Please note that I will be leaving home on the next big ship for a very long journey.
Please take care of my cacti, and make sure not to water them too much.
It makes them glum.
Farewell!
...
ZZZZZZZZZZ
AAAH!

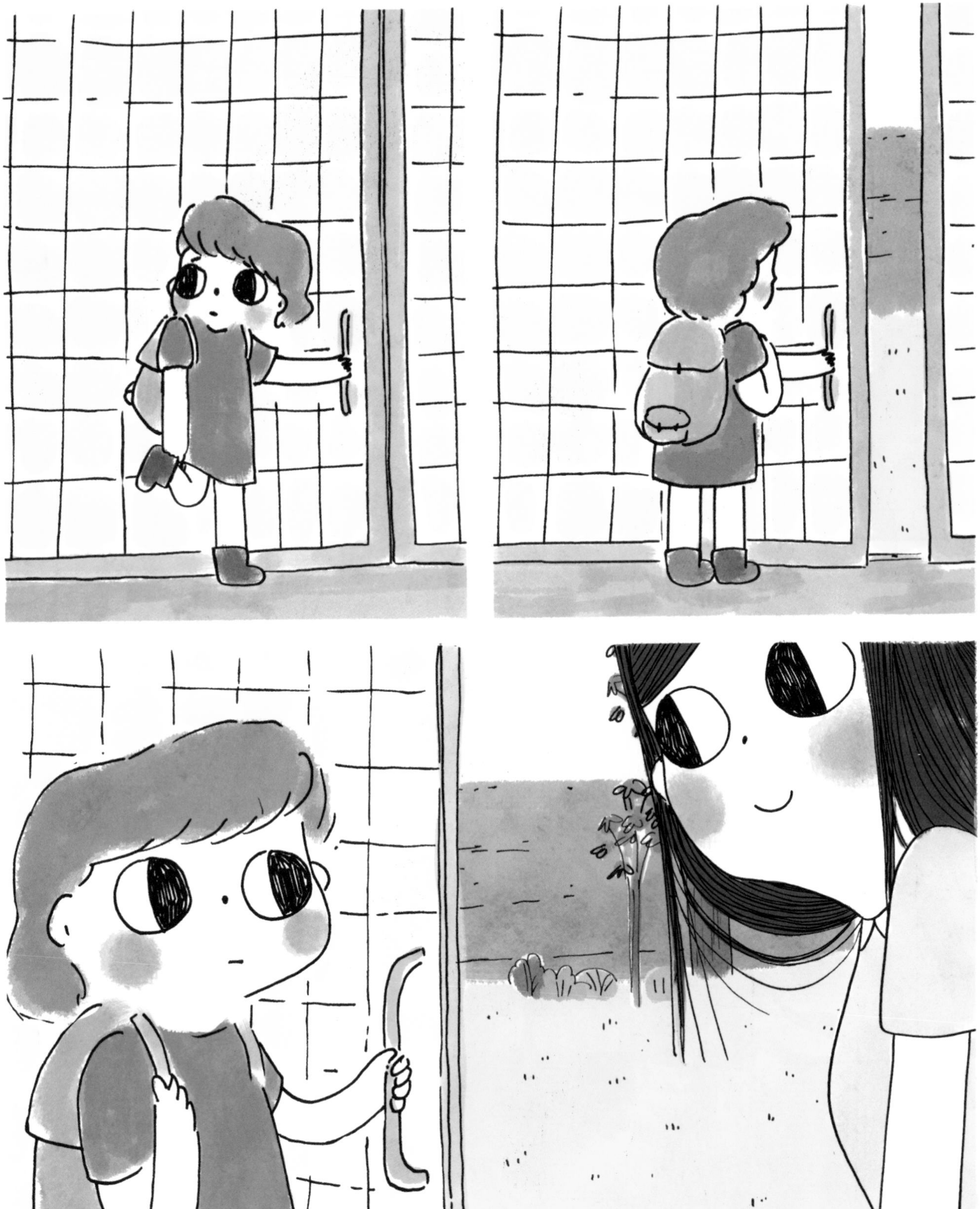

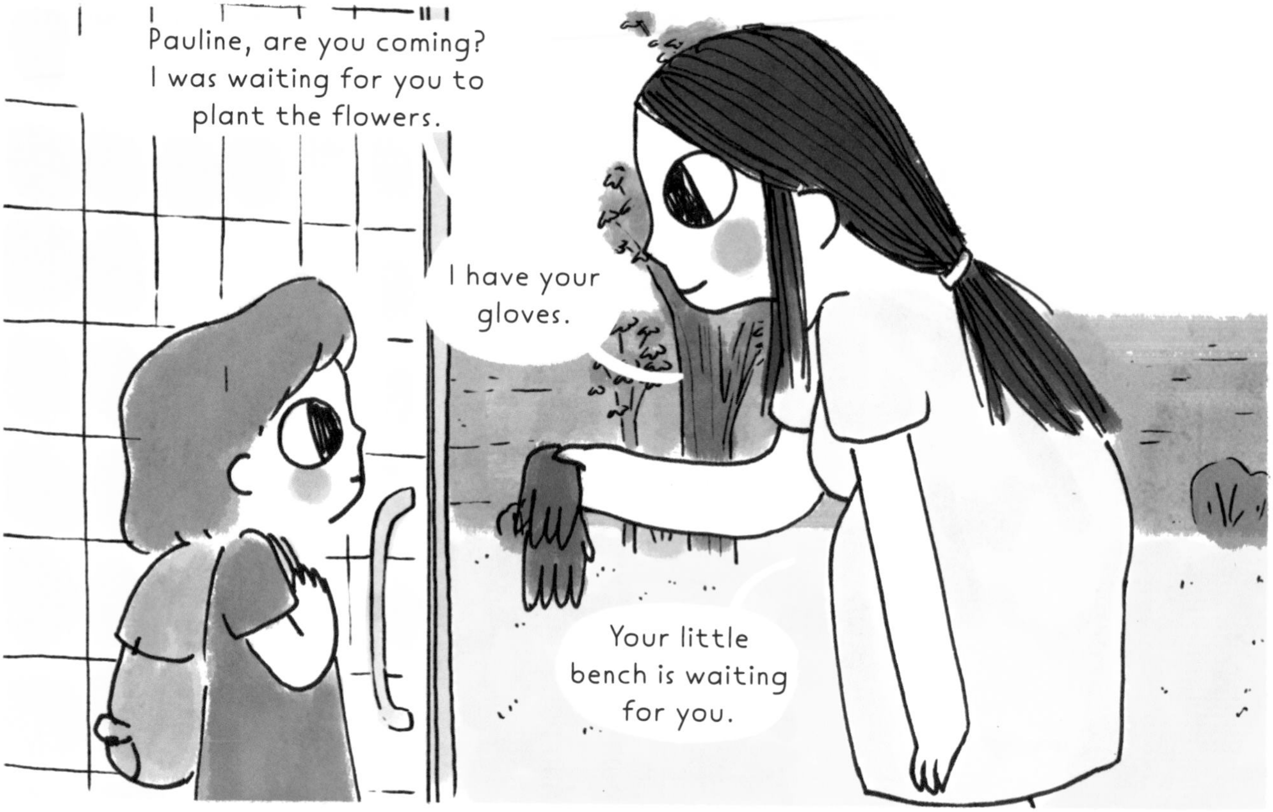
Pauline, are you coming? I was waiting for you to plant the flowers.
I have your gloves.
Your little bench is waiting for you.

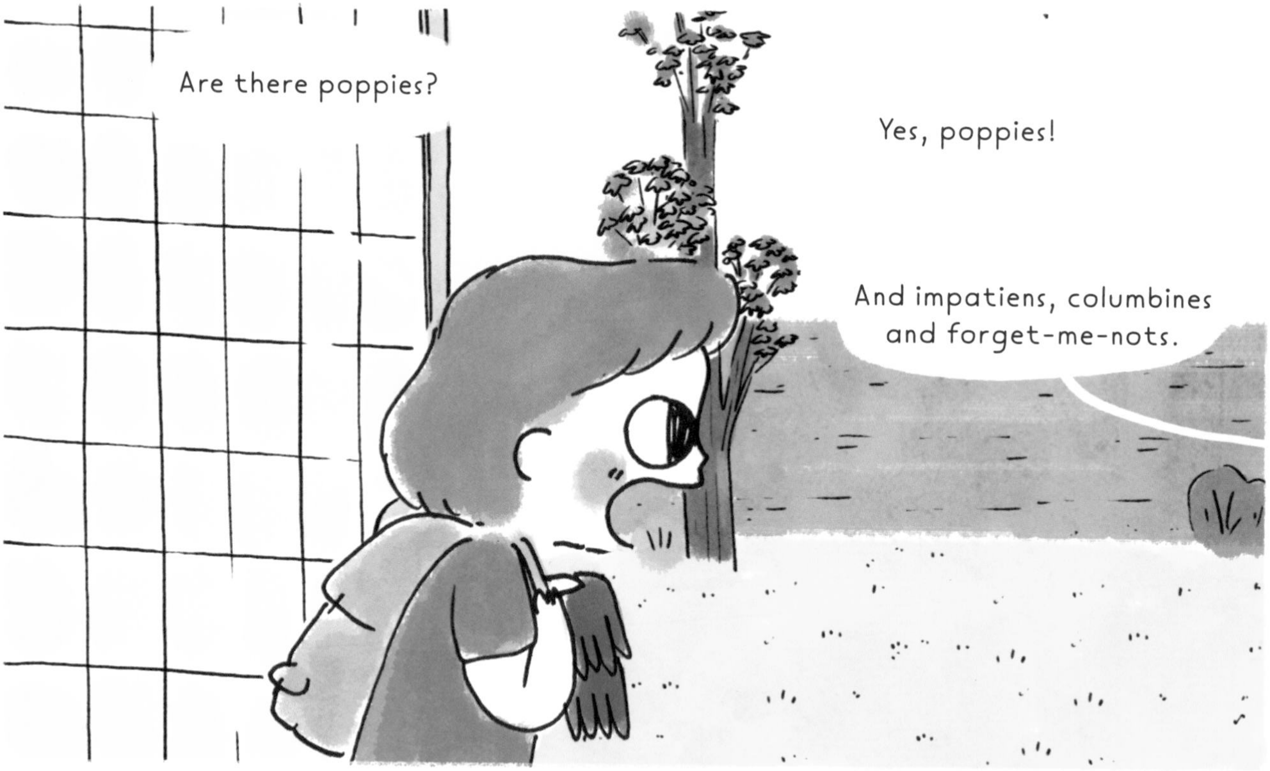
Are there poppies?
Yes, poppies!
And impatiens, columbines and forget-me-nots.

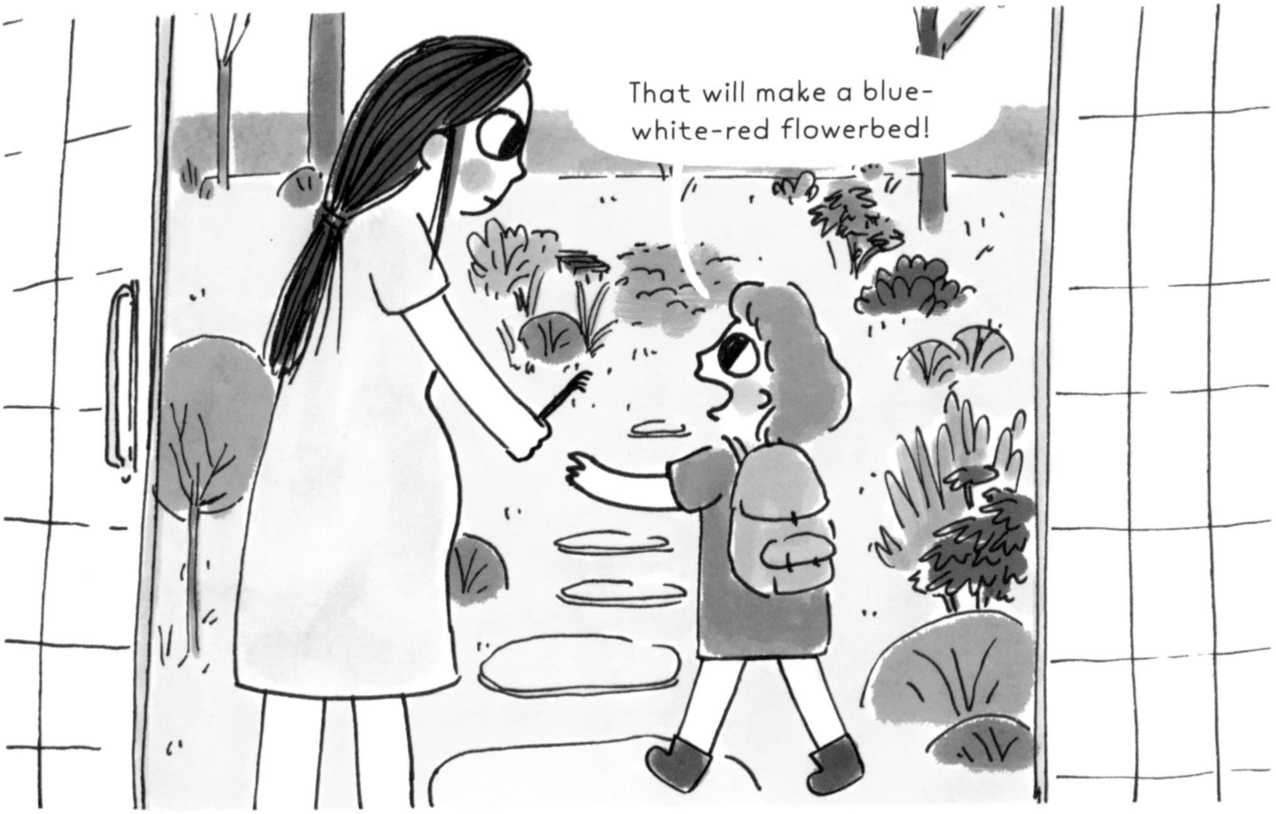
That will make a blue-white-red flowerbed!

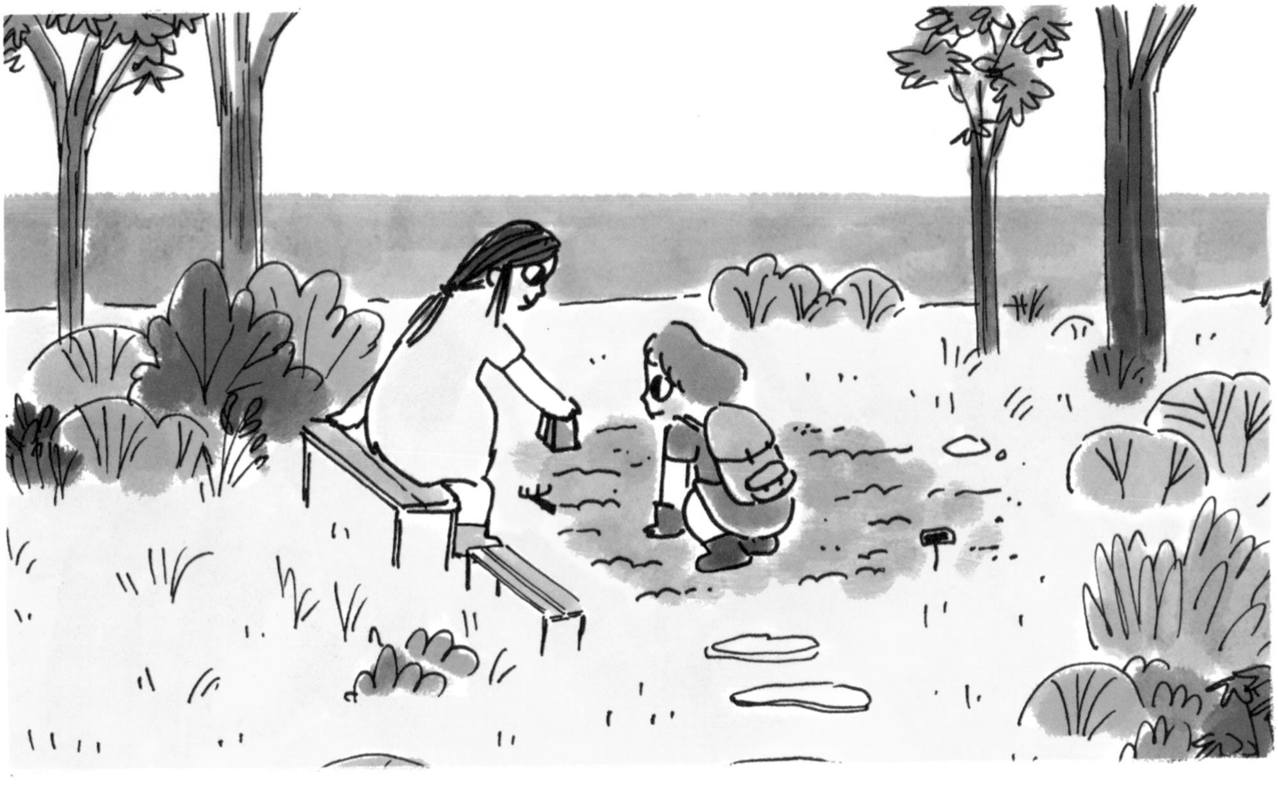

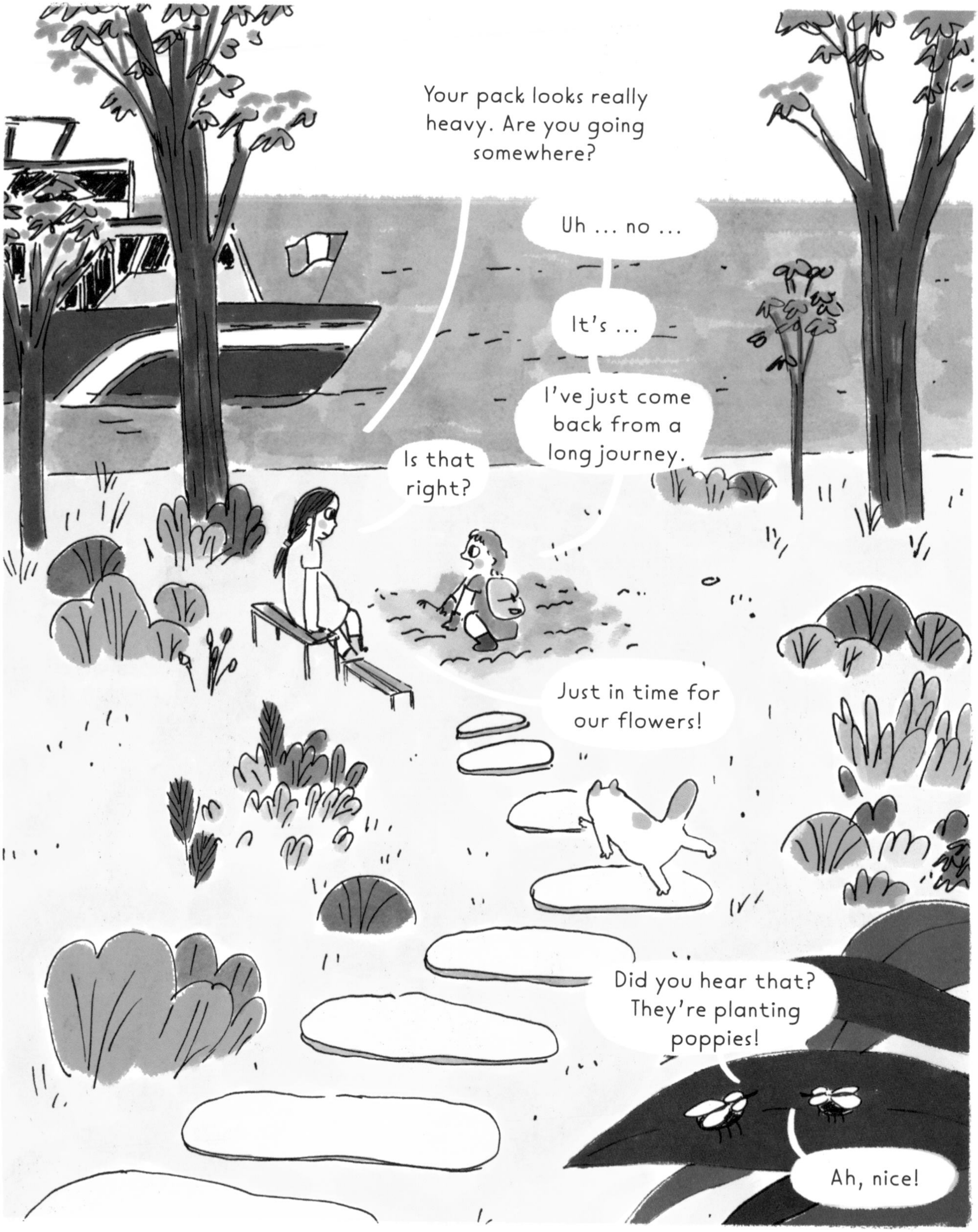
Your pack looks really heavy. Are you going somewhere?
Uh ... no ...
It's ...
I've just come back from a long journey.
Is that right?
Just in time for our flowers!
Did you hear that? They're planting poppies!
Ah, nice!

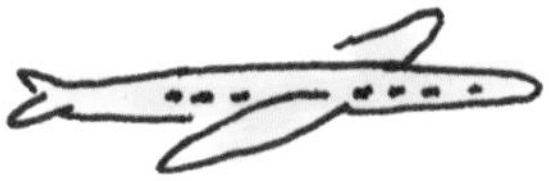

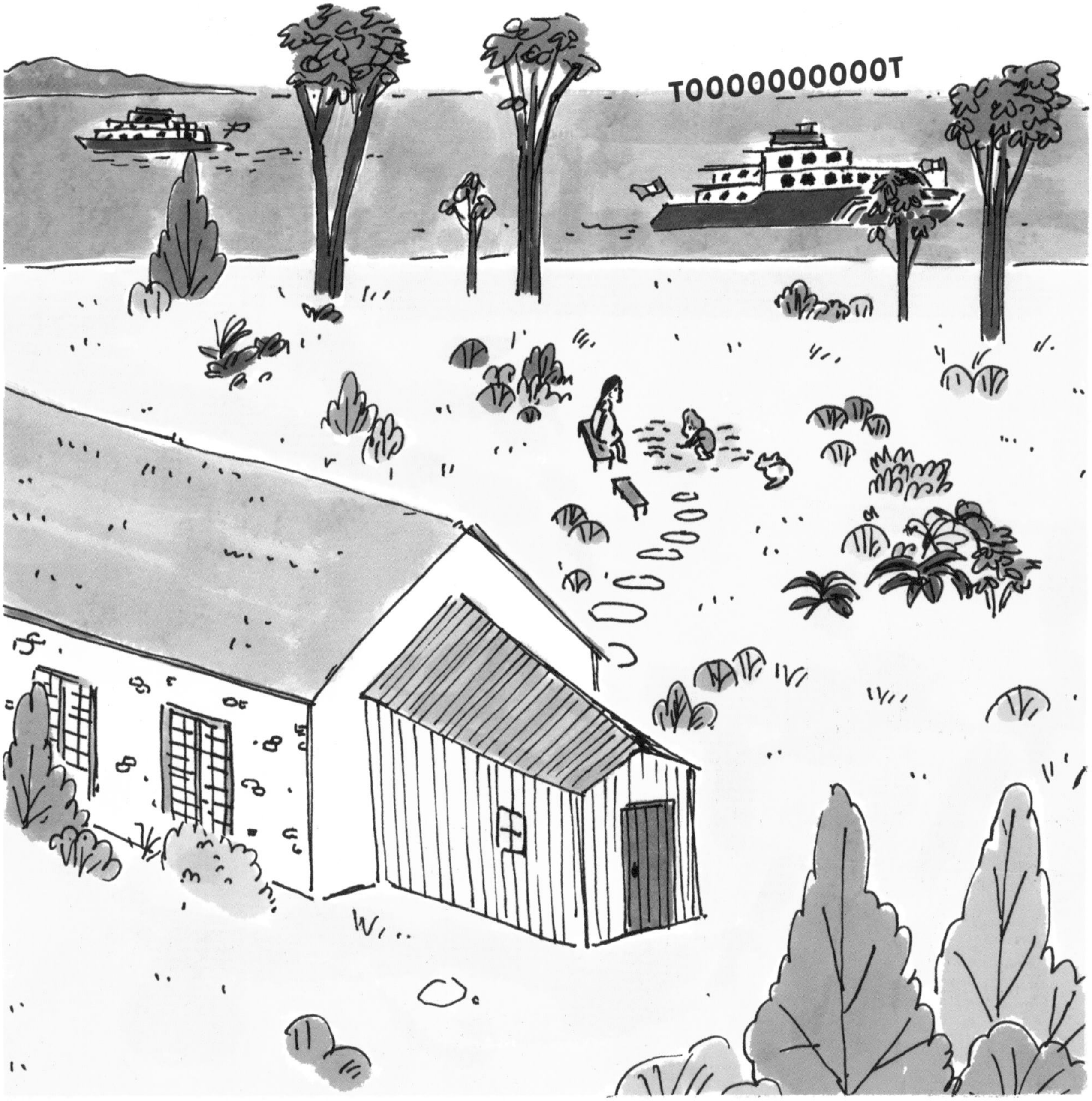
TOOOOOOOOOOT

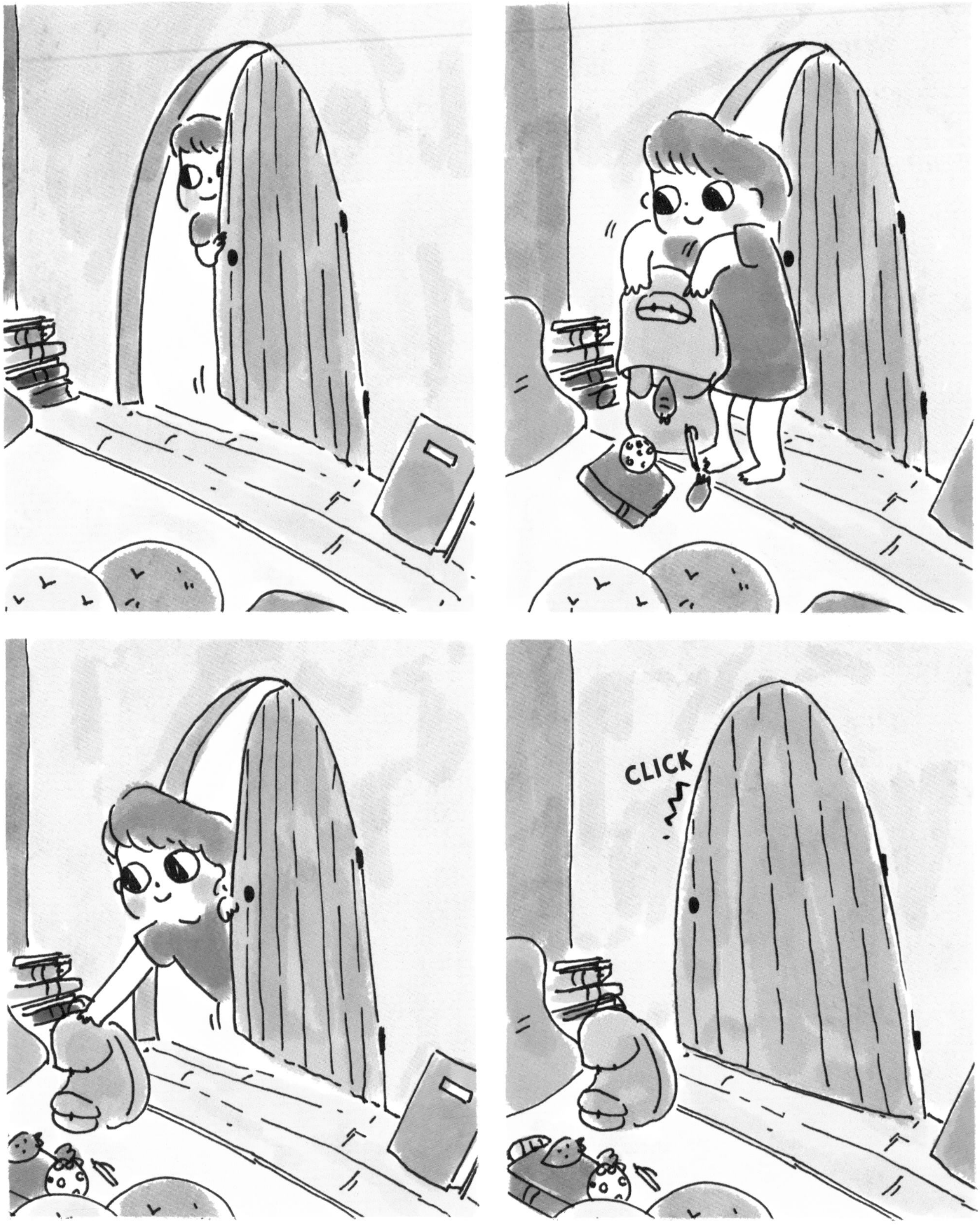
CLICK

The End

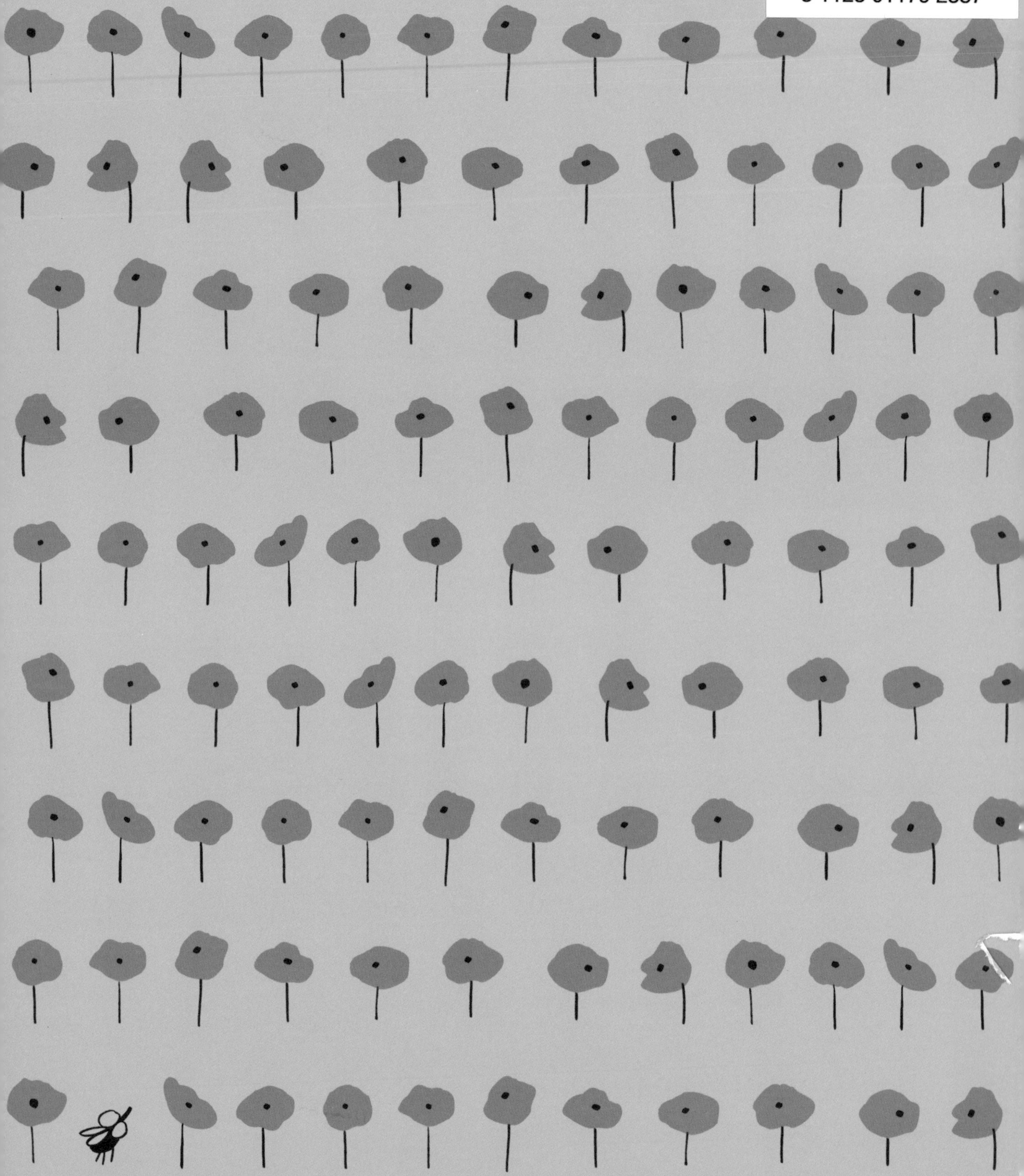